I0760879

Solineus

Sundering the Gods: Book 2.5

by

L. James Rice

TWELFTH
STAR

Solineus is a work of fiction. Names, characters, places, and incidents are the product of the author's imagination or are used fictitiously. Any resemblance to actual events, locales, or persons, living, dead, undead, possessed, or anywhere in between is purely coincidental.

Published by Twelfth Star Publishing, Council Bluffs, IA, USA

Cover design by Damonza.com
Cartography by Jenna Jing Rice

ISBN: 978-1-951068-02-8 paperback
ISBN: 978-1-732408-38-8 e-book
ISBN: 978-1-951068-01-1 hardback

Join the Sundering the Gods newsletter list for updates, promotions, and exclusive short works at:
sunderingthegods.com

Dedicated to my father and uncle, the two original story-tellers in my life, may their spirits have found the Conqueror Heaven.

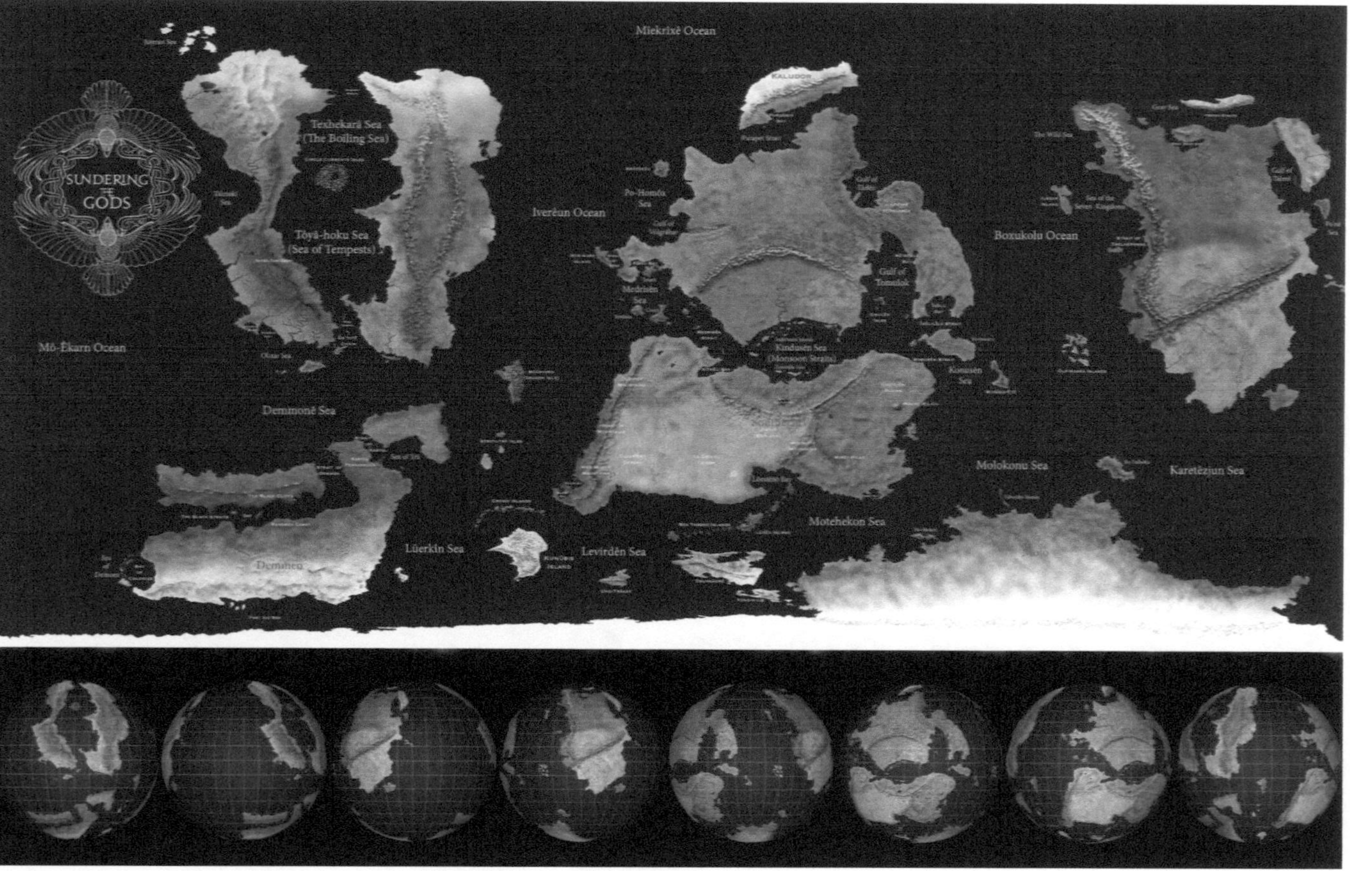
SUNDERING THE GODS
Miekrixè Ocean
Texhekarā Sea
(The Boiling Sea)
Tōyā-hoku Sea
(Sea of Tempests)
Mō-Ēkarn Ocean
Demmonē Sea
Ivereun Ocean
Po-Homēu Sea
Medrisēn Sea
Kaludor
Gulf of Tamulok
Kindusēn Sea
(Monsoon Straits)
Konusēn Sea
Boxukolu Ocean
Molokonu Sea
Karetēzjun Sea
Motehekon Sea
Levirdēn Sea
Lūerkin Sea
Kunobis Island

TERRITORY OF THE CLAN CHOERKIN

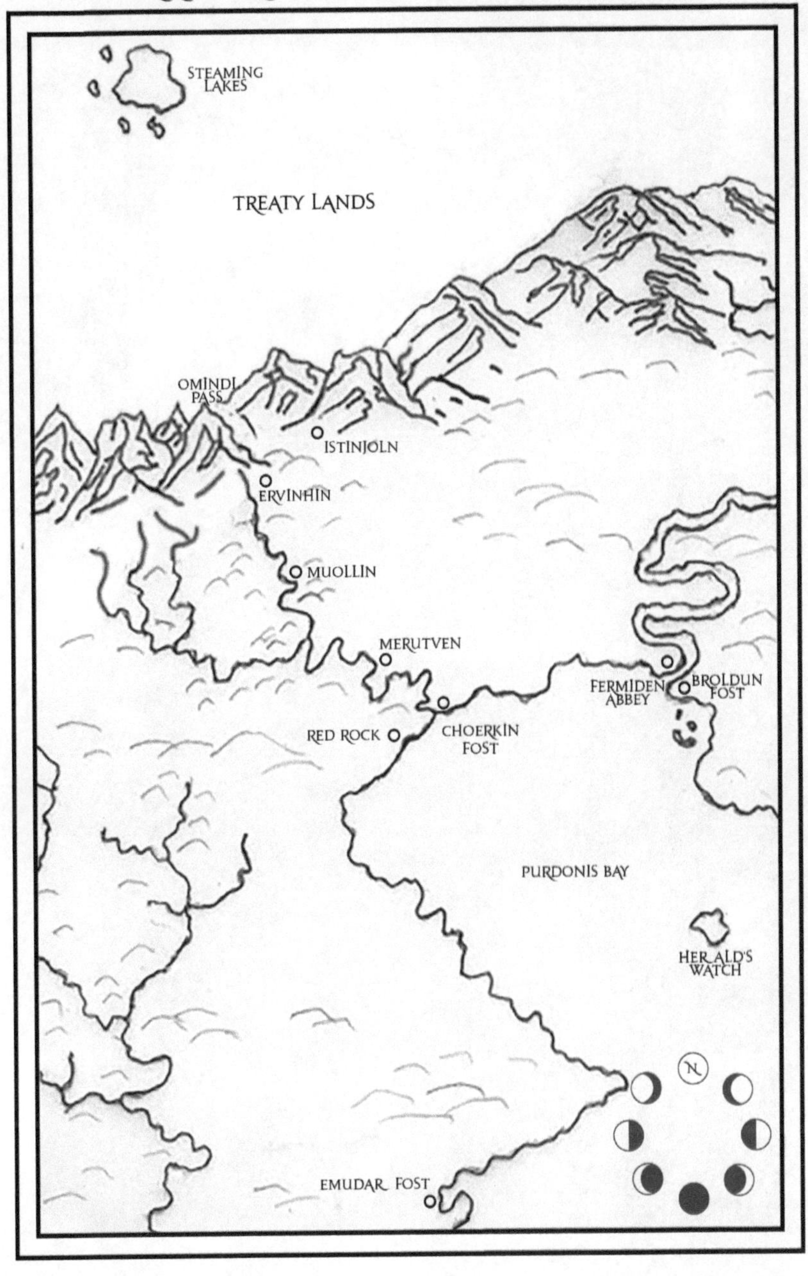

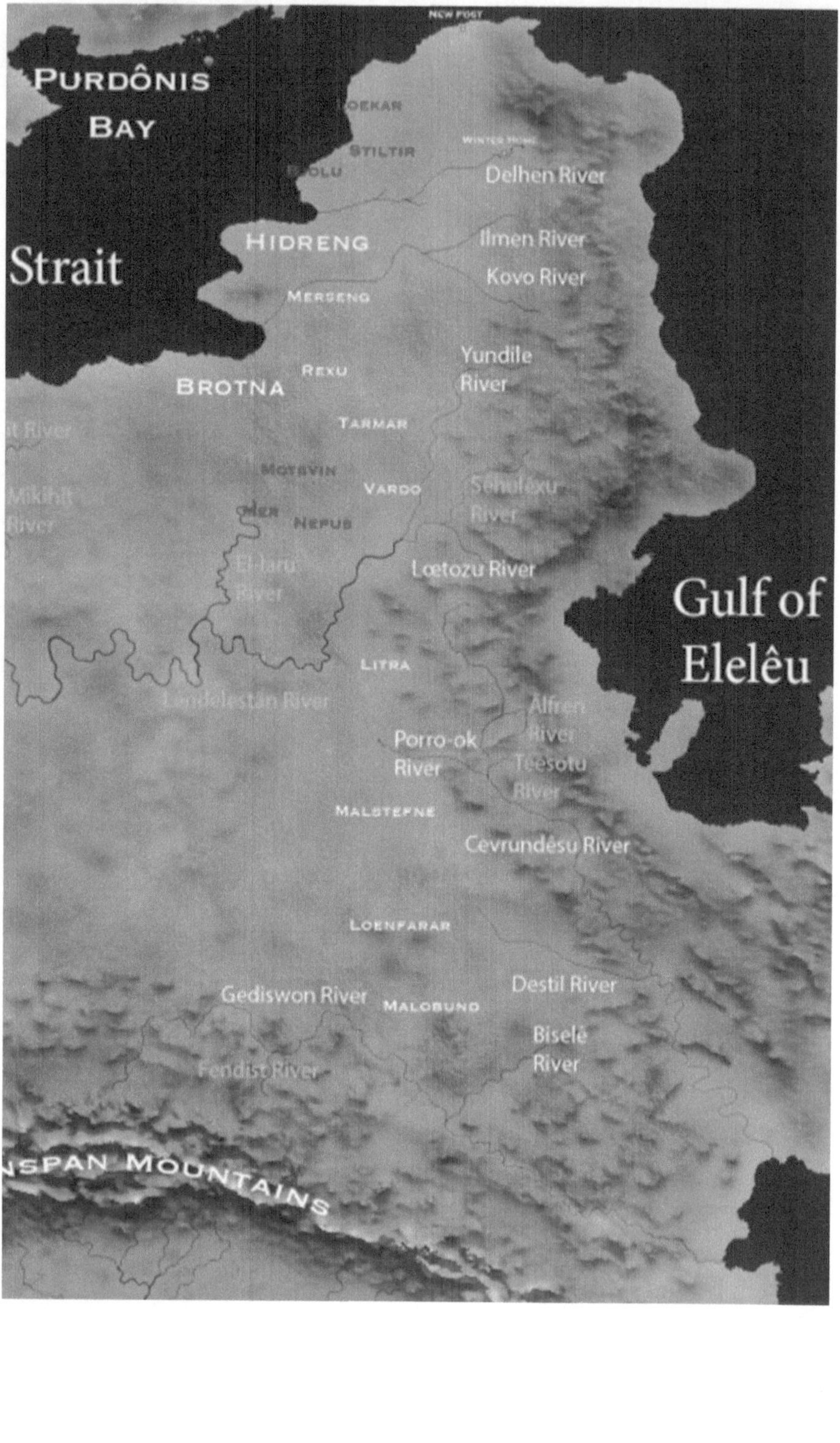
NEW POST
PURDÔNIS BAY
STILTIR
WINTER HOME
Delhen River
HIDRENG
Ilmen River
Strait
Kovo River
MERSENG
Yundile River
REXU
BROTNA
TARMAR
MOTSVIN
VARDO
NEPUS
Lœtozu River
Gulf of Eleleû
LITRA
Porro-ok River
MALSTEFNE
Cevrundésu River
LOENFARAR
Gediswon River
MALOBUND
Destil River
Biselé River
Fendist River
MOUNTAINS

THE SUNDERING THE GODS SAGA

EVE OF SNOWS
MELIU
TRAIL OF PYRES
SOLINEUS
CITY OF WHISPERS

Join the Sundering the Gods
Newsletter At:

www.LJamesrice.com

Signed Editions Available at
L. James Rice's Facebook page, or email:
LJRice@SunderingTheGods.com

If you enjoy Solineus, please consider
leaving a review at your favorite
online retailer.

ONE

A Curious Hand

I feint in the light of the shadow of myself,
a dearth of hope, a dirge for freedom,
a Soul a splinter's blink from the black of the eye.
Just try to ask why; prepare for the lye,
the burn, the scald, the scar.
Permanent nothing.

—*Tomes of the Touched*

Death is not for you, my love.

Solineus' eyes flittered open to a world of rolling, wispy blues, and he held the suspicion he bobbed in the river dead, no matter her encouraging words. "Why is that? Am I not mortal?"

Laughter. The Lady came to him like a puff of steam from a kettle: hazy, insubstantial, but real and warm. "You've washed against a fallen tree, and in a few moments a man will drag you from the river."

"Dead would be easier."

"Are you so set in your beliefs? May the immortal soul not be vulnerable to an eternity of torture?"

Solineus grunted, and maybe he frowned… or maybe it was just a branch of tree striking his face as he floated. Nothing in the blue universe was certain. "You've a way with making a man feel better about himself. Who do you want me to kill this time?"

Strands of the Lady's hair tickled his face as she leaned over him. "I only asked you to kill once."

"Funny how much killing I've done without killing that one. I need to get back to Kinesee, my people."

"Your people will cross the Gediswon and move south to safety, thanks to you. Fear of the Kingdomers and the Helelindin, and the threat of war between the Hundred Nations, will keep them at bay for a time."

"A war?"

Her smile was beautiful in its self-satisfaction. "The Malstefne rampaged through Malobund territory in your pursuit… this *will* have consequences."

"The more you talk, the more I reckon you want something from me."

Her breath warmed his neck as she appeared by his side, the Lady before his eyes fading. "The Silone people need friends; you are the man to lay such a path with the Eight Kingdoms and beyond."

"The hells you say. Kinesee, Alu—"

"The Trelelunin woman?"

"Aye, Lelishen. I can't leave them all behind."

"You may serve all their better ends, but it is a choice you must make. All I ask is to consider my words." Her breath landed in the shape of lips on the bridge of his nose.

"Tell me your name. If not, tell me who I am."

She giggled, puffs of heat on his neck and face. "I won't tell you who you were, but who you are and who you will be awaits you far to the west, in Kônu Bay. But, this you will know to be so only if you do as I ask."

She kissed him on the forehead, and a wet hand slapped and grasped his forearm.

Breath returned in a rush to his lungs and his eyelids burst open to a blue sky with veils of blowing clouds. His back drug on rock and his feet trailed in water; he hacked and coughed icy river water, and for a split-flicker his memory took him back to Bloody Boulder and the raper he'd dropped in the stream, and he wondered if some cosmic revenge hadn't switched their roles. His voice came with a gasp: "Rinold."

His body dropped to the bank, and a big-toothed smile loomed over him with a long beard braided with silver and brass rings. Morik spoke in Edan: "I will take you to your people when they return."

Solineus sputtered, spitting water. "What the hells are you doing here?"

"A fine greeting." He laughed. "I told you, I like booms! Dropping a bridge, this is something I didn't want to miss. And you, surviving the river? A very lucky man."

"Takes more'n a little water to kill me." Solineus took deep breaths. "The Malstefne army?"

"Turned back, but a few are on this side of the river." A quarrel clattered on rocks a stride from the Kingdomer's head, and Solineus gazed over the Gediswon; a Tek put toe to the nose of his crossbow and levered to reload while two dozen more slid from their horses.

Solineus followed Morik, both men scrambling up the bank. "Thought they turned back!"

"I might've been wrong!" He laughed and ran as shafts rattled grass and thunked the turf around them.

Solineus' body ached as they ran hunched over in zig-zag lines until the grasses grew so high seeds slapped his cheeks. A toe clipped a stone, and he tumbled down a shallow, rocky ravine, coming back to his feet with a hop. Several incoming quarrels arced through the sky, but they fluttered the grass thirty or more strides short.

He flopped on his ass and leaned against the rocky bank, smiling at the sky, gasping for breath.

Morik chuckled and slapped his shoulder. "Good fun, yes?"

Solineus glanced, pointed at the shield covering the man's back, linden wood and bound with iron; the bolt sticking from it was near center straight below his head. "You've got yourself a passenger."

Morik grunted with a twitch of curiosity on his face, slung his shield from his shoulders, and twisted the broadhead free. "You might want a shield yourself. Dual swords is a fine thing *after* the quivers go empty."

The Twins might take it as an insult. "I'll consider it. Where the hells did Rinold and the others get to?"

"Your people were forced west but had a strong lead. This is a good thing."

"My friends being hunted by Tek is a good thing?"

"Indeed. The Malstefne will know my people are not responsible for the bridge, and you and me are free as griffins to fly from here." He offered his hand. "An opportunity we should take."

Solineus clasped his forearm and stood, his head spinning with newfound altitude and his heart pounding from the pain through his chest and shoulders. "Tell me you brought a horse."

A straight-lipped smirk: "One horse, yes. Come."

They strode up a steep bank following an animal trail with thick brush for handholds. Glances from the top of the washout proved no one in sight, and when he looked back, three columns worth of bridge lay in the river.

Morik broke into a trot southwest and a quarter horizon later they stood in a second washed out ravine with rocky walls and floor, so hidden he didn't know it and the horse were there until they were strides away. The Kingdomer stroked the horse's neck then sat, leaning into the bank. "Wait to see if your friends pass?"

Judging by how the man looked to be settling in for a nap, Solineus figured that'd already been decided. He sat on a patch of dirt amid the rock. "Risky to come alone."

"More of my kin came to watch the bridge, no doubt they're hidden about, but I like to feel the shake in my boots.

Lucky for you. We should rest, make quiet, so we don't miss your friends riding past."

If they live. Solineus leaned against the bank and listened, but his thoughts meandered to the Lady and her words, and he couldn't keep his lips shut. "The Malstefne rode through Malobund lands, you think the Malobund will retaliate?"

Morik puffed his mustache. "One Nation likes little more than killing another. It is an insult to their king… it could mean war."

If the Lady spoke the truth… "I would like to meet your king. After all this."

An eyelid crept open. "Dark Waters take me, no. I pulled your drenched carcass from the river, it don't make us brothers."

The stern tone caught him off guard. "Well… Seems to me we're neighbors, seems to me you might want to learn something about us. Our language."

Morik rose to a knee with a huff and pointed to a snow-tipped peak in the distance. "See that mountain?"

"Near where we met?"

"The same. That is my mountain—"

"Your mountain?"

"My mountain: Shuntiskâ. You see that great mountain far back there? It is Molikîn, one of the Twenty-Two Foundations and home to Sînhôlar the Ironwing, King of the Helmvilîn, mightiest of the Eight Kingoms. What is it the Edan would say… I'd rather walk the Great Unrest than present you to my king and explain how I let a bunch of foreigners into our mountains and *then* explain how I gave you stonebreakers to destroy a Malobund bridge. In person? My king is wise and will not kill a messenger, unless the message is the messenger's fault, you see what I mean?"

"You plan to keep the bridge a secret?"

Morik turned and poked him in the chest, which hurt way more than it should after damned near drowning. "I intend to send a message attached to a keg of *your* whiskey. With a couple hangovers and his crown dunked in ice, he'll have had time to forgive me."

"Still, I think it'd—" The sound of hooves in the distance echoed and he stared north towards the river, but by the time his ears picked the direction, Rinold, Puxele, and Edlmir thundered past to the south with a riderless horse on their tails. "Rinold!" He jumped up and down, but there was no way in the hells they could hear him.

"Shut your mouth, I doubt they're riding alone."

Fresh dust rose in the west, and this time it veered their way. "Too late."

Morik grunted, stepped to his horse, and pulled a heavy windlass from its loop on the saddle and loaded a quarrel. "How many you see?"

They closed fast, but a count was more guess than fact. "Seven, I think."

"The *fômo* are on Helm dirt, so I'm obliged to try'n kill them."

Solineus squinted into the distance and the Twins hummed in his hands as the blades slipped from their sheaths. "Shits, more riders behind them."

Morik turned to him. "Stay alive, Mikjehemlut." His eyes turned to the Twins. "Eyes of Môgandar, man! Who are you to wield such blades?"

"I don't know." The cloud grew into thunder and Malstefne battle cries, their swords leveled at them. Morik still stared at the Twins instead of the Tek; Solineus pointed. "The enemy is that way."

Morik couched the butt of his crossbow and the twang disappeared in the charge's tumult, but a Malstefne rider leaned and dropped from the saddle. The Kingdomer hung his crossbow on its saddle-hook, slung his shield from his back and pulled a small ax from his belt. "As I was saying! Stayin' alive is the key to survival!" He laughed, and with a single step threw his axe.

The head flipped through the air but it was the haft that pegged a rider's cheek and rocked him in the saddle. Morik planted his feet and unhooked a bipennis ax from his belt.

And the riders were on them in a pounding rush of hooves, horse-flesh, and steel.

Solineus side-stepped and slashed a man's leg, but the horses didn't race by, the riders reined, spun, and hooves struck for his head even as he deflected a blade. He leaned from another blow, but the twirling rump of a second beast knocked his shoulder and he stumbled, then dove to avoid the edge of a curved sword.

A shod hoof clipped his ribs and he rolled, the warhorse prancing and stomping fingers from his chest and head, and a rider swung low in his saddle to bring his saber to bear.

Solineus scrambled and rolled to a knee, pain surging in his calf where a horse must've caught him. The Twins screamed in unison. One blade caught the Tek's sword, notching deep into the steel, and the other flicked the horseman's head from his shoulders.

The horse spun as the Tek tumbled from the saddle, its rump bouncing Solineus into the turf. His shoulder slammed into a grassy mound, hooves trampled around him, and the headless Tek's horse rolled with dead weight in its saddle. He slid close to the corpse and snagged the flailing animal's reins, and with a surge the beast rose; Solineus wrapped an elbow on an "ear" of the saddle meant to hug the armored rider's hip, and with a heft swung himself onto the horse's flank before lifting himself into the seat.

The Twins hissed amid a thundering crash of horseflesh and steel as shorter, heavy-set horses drove into them. He yanked the war horse's reins to see bearded men in mail swinging war hammers: Kingdomers. He jammed his heels into the horse's ribs and the beast kicked, launching a Malstefne warrior from his saddle, but satisfaction hammered into pain as a hoof caught his thigh and hand. He kept his grip with throbbing fingers, and the second Twin shrieked in his right ear; he caught the spear, redirecting it under his arm, then lunged the blade through the man's chest.

Horsemen broke from the fray, three Malstefne in flight, one with a war hammer's spike sticking from the steel plate he wore on his back. Five Kingdomers gave chase.

Morik turned and planted his feet to stare up at Solineus; blood streaked his chest and arms, and an abrasion shaped much like a horse's hoof bloomed on his cheek, promising to swell and turn black. "How in the name of the Five Earls did you get up there?"

Solineus cocked his head, smirked. "What else was I supposed to do? You only brought one horse." He nodded to the Tek and their pursuers. "Those men from your mountain?"

"Yes. It won't go well for the Malstefne, Ritik wants his hammer back."

Solineus chuckled as his new horse snorted, stomping to join in the chase. "One of them horses left you quite a beauty mark."

The Kingdomer rubbed his face and wiggled his jaw. "A cleaner hit and it would've put me in my tomb. Seems we both got lucky today. But at least you've a horse, save you the walk back to your people."

"Aye. I reckon." He patted the horse's neck, scratched beneath its mane. "I'd still like to meet your king."

Morik groaned. "Horse's kick might've softened my head, but... I'll take you as far as Yurhol to visit a smith I know there. Not often a man gets to see Ikoruv and Latcu together."

"In exchange for visiting your mountain, I will teach you the language of my people." Solineus proffered his hand. "The first word is 'friend'."

Morik grunted and didn't accept his hand. "In the language of Helm we say: *Carhôn maharôk tû.* Meaning, a pain greater than a kick to my hungover gut. What words do you have for that?"

Solineus' brow arched with a squint. "Pain in the ass."

Morik nodded with the Edan translation. "Pain in the ass, like a thorn? These are good words to fit you. I will take you to the village of Yurhol and send a message to my king. He will decide, and if he says 'no,' then you ride back to your people and far from me. Far, far."

"So far I can't bring you the whiskey?"

"Not so far as that." Morik shook his hand and spoke in Silone. "Pain in the ass friend."

❦ ❦ ❦

They rode for two days with an escort of ten Kingdomers. These others wanted nothing to do with Solineus, not so much as speaking a word to him.

Yurhol sat in a lush green valley which would've seemed a paradise on the island of Kaludor. Wild flowers, hundreds of hues of red and orange and yellow, followed the sun with their black eyes, and trees grew straight and tall. The village rested behind stone walls two poles high and three strides thick, and two square towers stood as the gatehouse. For a village which housed maybe a half a thousand souls, the defenses were formidable, a far cry from the village palisades on Kaludor.

Solineus spent every day of the last three weeks by Morik's side, and when this wasn't possible, he wandered to listen and interact with other folks to pick up as many words as he could. He and Morik both made strides in understanding the other's language, and it wasn't long before they could hold simple conversations in either tongue, so when Morik arrived with a message he spoke in Silone. "A Choerkin has offered to meet me at the Roemhien Pass to talk."

Solineus stood, adjusting the straps on a steel breastplate just finished for him by Yurhol's master armorer. It was far from the fanciest he'd seen in town, but Morik promised the steel was of the utmost quality. Mail would've felt more natural after months of living in the rings, but the Kingdomers insisted he adjust his fashion sense. "Which Choerkin?"

"Ivin Choerkin, Warlord of the Seven Clans... and his fiancé, one Kinesee Mikjehemlut. A relative?"

Solineus blinked. "Fiancé?"

"Her father! I can see it in your eye!" And Morik laughed, slapping his knee.

Solineus turned his eyes to the stone floor and scowled. "She's too young... But, I've no doubt neither of them is pleased with whoever made the arrangement." No doubt Meliu was irritable as well.

The Kingdomer wiped a tear from his eye. "I've heard you mention this Choerkin before, a good man. What is it he wants?"

The thing all Silone wanted was peace, a chance to recover their collective breath, but they had that now. "Bringing his *intended*, I reckon he's extending his hand in friendship."

Morik switched to the language of Helm. "But no doubt he wants something."

"Passage over the Roemhien… And knowing his mind, a defensible wall across the pass."

"You still believe your people will move south over the Dragonspans?"

"It's the only direction we've got, the valley will grow cramped soon enough."

"I will send a pigeon to Molikîn, let my king know what you anticipate. We should have an answer before we ride to Roemhien."

"You ride without me. I will ride to visit your king."

Morik grumbled. "He declined. It is time for you to go home. Don't you want your daughter to know you live?"

"She knows."

Morik eyeballed him. "She can't *know*. She may be as optimistic as any child, but no way she knows."

Solineus lowered his gaze, but kept his eyes locked with Morik's. He smiled. "A wager."

"You enjoy losing gold?"

"I'll ride with you, but I will stay hidden. You ask her whether I'm alive or dead. If she says anything other than I'm alive, I will return to my people. But, if she knows, you send me to your king."

Morik scratched his beard. "Not enough."

"She'll also know that I'll be back when she needs me."

"She will say that?"

"Aye, that's the wager."

"And if she doesn't? You leave, go home." He rubbed his nose. "I feel I'm about to lose a bet I shouldn't lose, but I accept."

Solineus shook Morik's hand. "When you send that pigeon to your king… you may as well let him know I'm coming to see him."

Morik laughed, but with an uneasy tone.

Five days later Solineus swung into the saddle amid an escort of Kingdomers, including Morik himself, their destination: The Royal Halls of Molikîn.

Two

Halls of the Ironwing

March to War and stumble to peace,
Bent Knee and Broken Back before the never humble priest,
in Telmener lies the waking and walking tomb,
the happy and talking doom-
Stretch the loom, the fibers never lost but impossible to follow,
search the words not knowing you're lost,
not knowing they ring cavern hollow.
Listen. To not hear.
To understand your own echo.

—*Tomes of the Touched*

The pigeons Kingdomers used to carry messages made the flight from Yurhol to Molikîn and back in a single day, but on horseback, the winding route with its rough, winding, climbing, and dipping trails, it took five days for Solineus to set eyes on the royal city. They passed a dozen goat herds along the way, as well as wagons hauling stone, raw ore, kegs, tanned leather, grain, and even bolts of bright linens Morik said traveled all the way from the Gorotan.

Although Solineus needed to remind himself that the Gorotan wasn't so far away as it used to be.

Turned out many of the mountains, if not every one, had a lord such as Morik, and goods from twenty or so of these mountains took this same road to Molikîn. Their little party drew plenty of stares from all these folks. Twenty-two armed Kingdomers with their Mountain Lord traveling with nothing more than a foreign man and a keg of foreign whiskey, no doubt these tradesfolk had reason to gawk.

Whereas Yurhol stood as a sturdy home and refuge against weather or attack, Molikîn rose from the side of a mountain as a fortress and city, perched above the valley below like some mighty bird. Four concentric arcs of walls met mountain cliffs and ended, each high above the other, with round towers jutting toward the peak above. From a distance it appeared a bit like Herald's Watch's big brother, but as they drew closer, he realized it was more comparing a man to a giant.

Massive blocks of white granite stood in places, tall as a man and twice as broad, but in others the walls rose carved from the mountain itself, so smooth even a squirrel would find challenge in gaining purchase. It wasn't a sprawling Tek city like Ivin described Bdein, but on entering a starker difference between this and other cities he'd seen and heard of struck him: The streets were wide and uncrowded. The merchant caravan they followed through cavernous gates had disappeared in the angles splitting buildings, and only a few dozen Kingdomers wandered the roads.

"I was expecting crowds."

Morik's saddle creaked as he turned. "Once there were, in the Age of God Wars, and there will be again once peace reigns longer than a generation."

Crowded or no, the buildings and streets were well kept. "War? Disease?"

The Kingdomer sighed. "Both, with certainty, but the reasons for most of those lost are forgotten. The Gods Wars are known as a bitter time—"

"These are not things for foreign barbarians," said a warrior riding nearby. "He should not think us weak because he sees so few here."

Solineus nodded. "Not my thoughts at all."

They passed through a stone gate which opened to a wide swath of green grass and trees crisscrossed by straight roads, in its center a bubbling pool of water; a natural spring, perhaps.

Morik scrunched his face and whistled before speaking again. "Tîern, these people are not our enemies, and they are the ones who are few."

"As you say, Mountain Lord."

"But I will judge my words before I speak them. We Kingdomers worship the Foundations... there were Twenty-Two gods in the beginning, but during the God Wars our enemies killed several of them, weakening our people, and so—"he tugged his beard and mumbled under his breath—"we were conquered and taken as slaves for a time. They say many were marched from their homes to the mines and forges of our enemies around the world."

Solineus leaned in his saddle as they passed through another gate and the road climbed. "A tragedy. My people have never believed in slavery." He didn't bother to mention how the Pantheon of Sol dealt with enemies in the Slave Fields.

"They took our mountains, razed the temples they could find, and populated our cities. Our masters, whoever they were, beat our gods from our souls, but the Foundations would not take defeat so easy. No. The priests and the people prayed in dark, hidden places. They prayed every day to Rînkodûl the Storm-Eye for freedom and revenge. Rînkodûl and the other gods gathered, and though too weak to face their enemy in pitched battle, they beseeched Bodomyûl, the Great Creator to which no mortal prays, to send the enemy away.

"But the gods did not know what fearful thing they asked for. Bodomyûl asked them three times if they were certain, and each time they answered yes! And Bodomyûl went to war, breaking the world, destroying our enemy in a Forgotten blink and banishing our enemy's gods from this world. But the lands changed, mountains tumbled, and the memories of men vanished."

It took Solineus several flickers to digest the tale being told. "The Great Forgetting."

"So many call it, but we of the Eight Kingdoms call it Bodomyûl's Wrath."

"The whole world paid the price for freeing your people?"

"The whole world paid the price for *enslaving* my people. Some question the wisdom of the gods, not because of the losses afflicted on others, but because His Wrath in turn banished our gods from returning to this world. But others say we would've been forever slaves, or our fires extinguished unto eternity if the decision hadn't been made."

Tîern said, "Some believe the Dead Gods—"

"Now who says too much?" Morik laughed, but the tone left no doubt to his hammering the man's mouth shut.

They rode in silence for a spell. The notion of some Great Creator breaking the world felt ludicrous, and no doubt neither the Edan nor anyone else prescribed to the same answer to this great mystery, but at the same time it intrigued him. Wherever there was an unknown, it seemed the human imagination filled the gap, whether fact, fancy, or something between. Didn't his own mind do the same? "I fear I'm not a pious man, don't know as I ever was. Not sure how I could be after…"

"From the tale you tell, it would be difficult for a man to forgive his gods. Perhaps you will find new gods in the Foundations."

Solineus laughed, but choked the humor and glanced about. "No offense to Rînkodûl nor a man amongst you, but any god and me would need a long chat before I bowed in prayer."

Morik's grin assured him no offense'd been taken. "The name Storm-Eye means Rînkodûl is the tranquility in the maelstrom; The Foundations welcome all who come in peace, no matter what faith they carry in their hearts."

"Much appreciated." He didn't doubt Morik's sentiment but questioned the range and depth of such a welcoming nature. Or perhaps, it was a weakness that their enemies exploited in a past age to take them as slaves. He ground his teeth; cynicism cut deep into his being by now, bleeding trust in a flow difficult to staunch. He needed a change of subject; he pointed to the highest walls in the distance. "Are we headed for the palace?"

"No. The First Throne of Molikîn will greet the Lords of Helmveline and our greatest allies. You will greet my king at the Third Throne."

Solineus chuckled. "So low, am I?"

Morik cast a sideways glance. "Gaining audience is an honor; it could've been the fourth throne, where my king meets with enemies… and pronounces executions upon the traitorous."

"I always loved the number three, anyhow."

Every street met another at hard angles in Molikîn, without a road winding or curving, which became all the more impressive as the roads climbed higher and steeper into the mountains. After a handful of turns and slopes climbed, they headed west down a broad road lined by shops, and the patrons wandered the streets. After a quarter horizon these folks disappeared, replaced by rows of breast-plated warriors standing rigid with halberds in hand, mail draping to their knees, and their faces hidden behind nasal guards.

A pyramid of stairs rose from the center of a broad courtyard with the gates to the second tier of the city framing its rising steps into an idyllic portrait. A symbolic mountain, he'd wager. Atop the pyramid stood a stone pavilion with a red-tiled roof, its ridges gilt in silver clouds with golden griffins marching their lengths; three shining beasts at each corner.

The stone stairs they trod were black granite polished to a sheen and dimpled with images of blooming vines and prancing goats. A handrail of red-gold led their climb, with posts knobbed with a steel-like metal, but its silver shine held a violet tint.

If this is the Third Throne, the First must be a dandy. He grinned to himself, but Morik squinted with disapproval as if he'd spoken aloud. "What?"

"The twist to your lip… recall that my king bears little humor for strangers he refused to meet the first time."

They strode to the top of what must've been a hundred steps, and here two guards in armor a deeper blue than an evening sky slid gold-gilt doors open. A polished white floor greeted them, carved and inlaid with a silvery metal, but a single path of silver-specked gray lead to two thrones sitting atop a white-marble boulder chisel chiseled into a thunderhead. A dozen warriors with halberds flanked the dais on either side.

A man with an unadorned black beard and black eyes stared straight past him as if Solineus wasn't there. A cloak fashioned from silk and the thick white fur of some animal draped his shoulder, clasped by a buckle and pin of gold shaped as an eagle's head. Beside him, and holding his right hand, sat a woman staring straight into Solineus' eyes, her hair more red than Meliu's, but her skin darker, and her face full and round. Crowns of gold, streaked with hues of red and violet, sat on their heads, each with eight points tipped by cut diamonds; the facets of the stones above their foreheads shimmered not unlike Kinesee's pearl when rubbed.

I reckon this is what a king and queen are supposed to look like... Kinesee would love this.

Morik led him to within ten paces of the base of the cloud-thrones, and they knelt with knees settling on silk pillows the green of a verdant valley shimmering with morning dew. Only then did Sînhôlar the Ironwing deign set eyes on Solineus.

The queen leaned into her husband's ear, then addressed them. "This is the foreigner my husband refused to greet?"

Morik touched his nose to stone in a bow with his hands at his hip before raising his eyes to the woman. "Queen Nisenî, Lady of the Fourth and Seventh Foundations, it is so. I beseech patience and forgiveness."

She raised her hand to cut his words short. "Bringing a foreigner to Molikîn uninvited, it seems to me you do not cherish your mountain home. The terms of your lordship approach renewal."

The notion of a lordship expiring brought blinks and an arched brow, but Solineus figured keeping his yap shut was wiser than voicing any questions.

"I am aware, My Queen."

"My husband met this people's request for passage and will negotiate fair terms for a defensible wall. What more do these barbarians wish?"

"My Queen, nothing more than to meet the two of you, who are so generous."

"There cannot be a proper meeting! Ironwing ears will not hear a barbarian's tongue spoken in Molikîn, nor speak to one who cannot understand the speech of the Holy Foundations."

It wasn't his turn to speak, Solineus knew it well, but he bowed until his nose touched stone, then raised his eyes. The bold path had served him well thus far. "I've a passing bird's knowledge of your language."

The Ironwing's stare didn't budge, but the Queen's breath caught in her throat, and she coughed. She glanced to King Sînhôlar then back to Solineus; her lips either suppressed a grin or a frown, with no way to be sure which. Morik, on the other hand, was not pleased. "My apologies for this barbarian, My Queen—"

Her hand cut Morik off a second time. "This foreigner is brazen. How have you come to speak so well in such short time?"

"I've a way… I can pronounce words before I know what I'm even saying."

"And a way of speaking before you should. What is it you seek, barbarian?"

"Negotiating terms for a wall." But the Lady's desire snuck into his head and slipped from his tongue. "Peace and trade with all Eight Kingdoms."

"The wall is between the Ironwing and the Warlord Choerkin to chisel. Peace is the nature of the Eight Kingdoms, but for many, trade with foreigners is rare, and we've no influence even if so inclined to speak for you. And we are not."

Morik said, "You are kind to point out—"

Solineus cleared his throat. "I ask for no influence other than safe passage."

The King didn't twitch, and Morik's stare was harder than the Queen's, but her words were measured and rough as pumice in tone. "Such guarantees are impossible. While the Foundations are at peace, a foreigner's head is bound to be lost in a thousand horizons of mountain trails."

"I've traveled further already with enemies determined to spill my blood, with the blessing of the Ironwing I will take this risk."

"The Ironwing gives no such blessings!"

A spirited laugh from the queen, humor and outrage in a tittering blend, but the Ironwing raised his palm. His voice came deep, resonating with authority. "There is a singular path, but it is not for a soft low-lander accustomed to sun and soft beds."

Solineus sucked his breath and exhaled; The Lady always seemed to get her way. "I hail from a land of mountains, not so high and grand as the Foundations, but with trails so cold as to freeze a man's eyes unblinking in his head."

"What gods do you carry in faith?"

Solineus squirmed. "None I care to name."

Queen Nisenî scowled. "Because you fear we know their names."

"No. Because I fear them. What faith I had is broken."

The Queen cocked her head with a judging squint, and the Ironwing spoke, his eyes pinned on Morik. "Is this so?"

"Impossible for me to judge a man's heart in truth, but from hearing his tale, I believe that before you kneels a godless man with no faith in his heart, a Pilgrimage of the Foundations may bring the peace of the Storm-Eye to his soul."

Solineus didn't know what the hells this pilgrimage he spoke of was, but it brought the queen to her feet. "Forbidden! Foreign gods may never walk the Foundations, carried by their pagan worshippers."

The Ironwing's hand rose. "This lady, who is the fire in my soul, speaks true, but if indeed your heart is empty and open, it may be proven so." The queen fumed. "The Twelfth Foundation defies all unworthy hearts."

Twelve Hells and a Twelfth Foundation didn't bring joy to his heart, but it was the queen's sudden calm and easy smile as she sat back in her throne that brought a queasy unease. Her cocksure tone stirred the butterflies further. "This is so. My King is wise."

Morik shook his head as Solineus met his gaze. "You must find another road. I don't wish to see you dead so soon after saving you."

Solineus breathed deep and stiffened his spine. "What is this Twelfth Foundation?"

"It is the highest mountain to hold a Foundational Shrine, ancient texts say it is dedicated to Armungrînd, known as the Griffon-Tamer, but no one since Pîlôstar the Skywind has reached its top. They say only a pilgrim favored by the gods can breathe the airs so high and pure without dying. It cannot be done."

The Ironwing spoke: "Pîlôstar rediscovered each of the Twenty-Two Foundations and their shrines and left a token atop each. The Helmveline hold five of these tokens as the first to reach them, more than any except the Kingdom of Barkûsh, who also hold five."

It seemed a truth of the world: Everybody, even the most wealthy and powerful, wanted something more. "And if I bring you this token?"

"It proves the favor of the Foundations rests in your heart, and the priests will bless your holy journey to cross the Foundations." He wiggled his fingers in a peculiar gesture that reminded Solineus of a humming bird. "This pilgrimage will bring you to every kingdom to see if you can keep your head while forging alliances. And of course… Announce my possession of the Twelfth's Token."

Solineus cocked his head, shrugged. "Show me this mountain and I will climb it."

The queen laughed, but the Ironwing spoke without a smile. "Before any Kingdomer may plea with this mountain's heights, they must cleanse their souls… a heretic and Barbarian such as yourself more so, to prove your worth. But before I decide whether to give you this chance, I will see the blades you bear."

He gestured for Solineus to rise, but he hesitated; Morik had warned him that once he kneeled, to not stand again in the presence of the Ironwing. He glanced to the side, but Morik's gaze was as uncertain as his own.

"Rise," said the king. "I am allowed to command my own laws broken."

The man's left cheek twitched toward his eye, the first hint of a grin from this man, and Solineus stood, striding forward. He slipped the swords, gripping them still in their sheaths, from their harness and kneeled when he drew close, extending his hand with a Twin in each. "I don't recommend touching them."

The Ironwing nodded without a hint of insult taken, and the queen squirmed in her throne, pressing as far from the Twins as her seat allowed.

"Place one before me and show me the blade of the other."

Solineus did as he requested, and the murmur of the Sister entered his mind with a peculiar sense of calm as he slipped the blade a hand's length from its home. *She doesn't fear this king?* Rare for a Twin to be so quiet.

The Ironwing leaned close, tracing his finger near where the blade's Latcu blended with the hilt's Ikoruv, but not touching. "Spirit bound, no doubt."

"They contain some life-force, aye."

"You possess them, but you do not understand them." The king grinned for the first time. "It is a common misconception amongst even the learned that a spirit resides in the blade… perhaps sometimes it is true, who is to know for certain? But it is more apt, the spirit is linked to the blade from the Celestial."

The Edan mentioned nothing of the sort, but why would they? They wouldn't believe he needed to know, if it was even true. "So, the spirit itself is not here?"

"Grandmaster Fezdal-Kîn teaches that the spirit-blade is much like an *onved.*"

Solineus scrunched his face. "This word I do not know."

The Ironwing leaned back in his throne. "I suppose not. An *onved* is a powerful stone, a magnet of a sort. A Master Wayfinder may place one of these stones anywhere in the world… Above ground, in the deepest mines, and no matter where the master travels, they will find their way back. Do I make sense?"

Maybe something like how he had a felt where Kineseee was whenever she rubbed the pearl? "I think it might. A bit like a way-stone and a mark on a map."

"Indeed, only the way-stone points to this single place *only*."

"You're saying the blade is an *onved,* so the spirit in the Celestial knows where to go?"

The Ironwing's head bobbed somewhere between a nod and shake. "It is more, it doesn't provide a mere destination, it provides a path."

"You believe the spirits… they're not here, but they're here? A constant connection."

"Ask yourself, does it feel they are more in the blades, or more within your own head? I do not know the answer to your question… perhaps they are in the Celestial as well as here with you and these blades? Two places at once. Maybe they travel back and forth. Maybe only a fragment of them ever leaves the celestial. Maybe they are never drawn into blades, but drawn into you when the swords are drawn? Should I know the answer, my name would be carved in the Mountain of Knowledge for all time. Do they speak to you?"

"Murmurs, whispers, shouts. Rare to recognize anything which might be a word…" The memory returned in a rush. "Gersvôresh'kûmjotu'kî. At the bridge, both swords repeated these sounds… these words. Do you know them?"

The man's brow knitted, and he sucked a breath through his nostrils. "No. But I will note it and inquire with our scholars."

Solineus nodded. "Gibberish, I'd wager, but I thank you for the effort."

"You may sheath the weapon." The Ironwing stood, placed a hand on Solineus' head, and spoke, his voice thundering to make certain everyone heard. "A man who bears such holy artifacts must be given a chance to prove his heart. This barbarian will purge his body and soul of all evil and ascend the Twelfth Foundation in the name of Helmveline, in the name of the Ironwing, in the name of all the gods we have lost. In one month's time, if our holy deem him cleansed, his journey shall begin. The Will of the Foundations lead his heart."

Solineus bowed, nose to the step in front of him as the queen rose, and the royal couple turned and left the hall. There he remained, snuffling stone and his eyes pinned on the brother until a hand grabbed his shoulder. He leaned back with a deep breath, hooking the Twins back into their harness.

"How's it feel to know you've a month yet to live?"

Solineus hopped to his feet with a grin. "Take more than a lit— a big ol' mountain to kill me."

Morik led him outside and started down the stair before speaking again. "It is never the mountain that kills a man, my pain in the ass friend."

Solineus chortled. "You are ever the font of optimism." He spoke in Silone: "Don't reckon the Ironwing will share that Broldun whiskey? Seeing as I'm about to die."

Morik squinted. "Depends on when your fasting begins."

Solineus stopped at the bottom of the pyramid. "Fast? As in not eating? I don't like not eating."

"I reckon, then, you won't enjoy the last month of your life."

Three

Mountain Tongues

Black Bell with the Hallowed Ring,
echo the wagging tongue
on fire.
Desire. Destiny. Doom.
The spinning wheel and the loom,
the forge and the bludgeoning hammer,
the spur to horse's canter.
Tongue dance to the last,
Death's gait a hop, skip, and prance.

—*Tomes of the Touched*

If three weeks of fasting achieved nothing else, it convinced Solineus that climbing and maybe dying on a mountain wouldn't be so bad. Standing on a rocky, wind-swept trail staring up at the damned thing brought pleasant reminiscences of gurgling pains in his gut.

"You're godsdamned shittin' me, right?"

They'd passed a hundred high peaks on the way here, though he got turned around so often he wondered if some weren't the same mountains from different views. But this thing, this behemoth, this giant with its snow-capped head raked by streaking clouds, was something other.

Morik scoffed. "Won't hurt my feelings if you change your mind."

No doubt; the man had spent every day for the past month trying to talk him out of it, if for no other reason than the Ironwing had commanded the Mountain Lord to forsake his mountain home in order to assist his pain in the ass friend. This left Tîern returning to Shuntiskâ Mountain as overseer until Morik's return, something the boy's family had dreamed of for decades, from what Solineus gathered.

"If I succeed, the king will extend your lordship through the lifetime of your eldest child."

"And if you die, I lose a thorn in my ass. I see how you might think I win on either account."

Solineus chuckled. "At least it isn't so cold, not yet." The base of the mountain was still green here, where soil perched between boulders and scree grew low grass and hardy trees. Only half way up the mountain's side did snow and ice appear, and the ridge took a slower rise than many they'd seen. "Don't look like I'll have to climb straight up, neither."

"There are far worse ascents… My people are more inclined to climb those peaks from the inside with pick and shovel, but this climb is a deception. The air up high grows maddening; the tongue can blather a fool's song or just tie in a knot like a drunkard. Then, you fall over and die."

"Everything ends in death for you, don't it?"

They shared a grin. "It does for all of us. No, if the climb was steep, I'd tie you to a post like a wayward ram, your lungs wouldn't take it."

They continued on after the leaders of their train of porters, forty Kingdomers laden with gear, food, and water, rounded a corner to catch up. Included in the group, three priests to bless the climb, and his body on the odd occasion it came tumbling back; most folks just stayed up there dead, frozen chunks of history.

The ridge which looked so damned straight from a distance turned out to be a twisting climb, but on the bright side, the trail was solid and clear of ankle-twisting rocks from all the pilgrims who'd come before them. Morik assured him that hundreds of Kingdomers made the climb every year, stopping at various points to pray, six camps in all, before deciding to turn back due to altitude or weather.

"How high have you been?"

Morik grinned. "Not so high as I'm going to take you. I was young on my pilgrimage to this mountain, and in love. I could've made Camp Zjindinfôk, the final before the summit, if I'd been willing to forsake a warm woman for another week or two, weather depending."

And there was the depressing truth of this journey: Weeks to climb a distance he could walk in a day without breaking a sweat. "Wouldn't prayer make the journey easy? Some kind of magic?" He imagined Eliles could handle this task with disturbing ease, with the Sliver of Star.

"It's been tried, many times, and folks still die. Two troubles, as I hear: The first is the devout use prayer early, and when they reach near the top and prayer fails for a moment, they aren't used to the peculiar air and die, but even if they prepare proper… Prayer takes focus? I don't know exactly, but—"

"They die."

"That's the short of the story."

"You're certain there's no critter up there just eating folks?" The notion of an Mokotu-xe elemental living atop the mountain wasn't encouraging.

Morik's head cocked and he shrugged. "It isn't unthinkable. But, Pîlôstar the Skywind didn't mention one in his journals."

They rounded a bend and smoke rose in the distance, sourced several hundred feet higher than they stood, and it looked like stone buildings rose from the mountain. "A village?"

"The Temple of Arumbor, carved into the face of the cliffs by the ancients, and a few buildings we Kingdomers added."

"And we'll be staying there a week?" When he'd heard of a camp at the base of the climb, he'd imagined pitching tents and fighting to get a fire started. "And we sleep inside?"

The Kingdomer laughed. "Aye, we sleep inside."

Despite how near it seemed, the winding, rocky trail dashed his hopes of a hot meal for several more hours, but reaching the gated entry was a joy. Men and women raised their arms, singing to their arrival, and Morik and the porters returned the song, so he joined in despite not knowing the hells he sang.

Most of the smoke he'd first seen rose from buildings perched atop a cliff face some forty feet high, with a robed figure standing atop the tower, but a dozen thin trails of smoke drifted from the ground like a fog rising after a rain on a summer day, from fires within the cliff's temple, he surmised. The face of the cliff was gray with streaks of dusky oranges, and the lower half stood carved with doors and windows, along with glyphs he assumed were holy text. The climb ahead might kill him, but its beginning was auspicious and comfortable.

A robed woman stepped from a door gouged from the cliff and she raised her arms in greeting. "The party from Helmveline? We've been expecting you."

Morik waved the porters to a door to the south and lead Solineus onward to the stairs leading to her. "Seblêsu, Lady of the Mountain, I am Morik, Mountain Lord of Shuntiskâ, and this is Solineus of the Emudar, from a land far to the north."

Seblêsu was a title Solineus interpreted as High Priestess, only with the specific meaning of her overseeing this Foundation. He bowed. "Seblêsu, Lady of the Mountain, it is with humility I stand before you and this mighty summit."

She stood straight, gazing down her nose. "It is most unusual for a barbarian to make the Foundational Pilgrimage. Not in my lifetime has such a thing occurred. The last was

Lodupûl of the Histê peoples, praise his tenacious name. Not even he attempted to reach the coin of Hîmr."

It was the first he'd heard of another "barbarian" making the pilgrimage. "The Histê?"

"A people who live far to the east and south of the Foundations. Heathens, heretics, and slavers who worship demons… But they say Lodupûl was not as his brethren, and he lived among the Kingdoms until his death."

Demon worshippers, I know an island they could visit. "The Foundations willing, I will retrieve the coin and return the treasure to the Kingdoms."

Her head bobbed. "I am a fool who believes every journey for the peak will be *the one.*"

"What happened to the last climber who tried?"

She smiled. "Four years ago… Has it been so long already? There were two, Lilquin of Kâmar and Reblôn of Barkush. I thought maybe they would work together and succeed; I shouldn't have been optimistic for either. Competition is no way to survive the dead airs of the summit."

"So, they died?"

"One must assume, as neither returned. Rumors from history speak of pilgrims who snuck back down the mountain to hide their shame, but these were men without fear."

"Everyone who tries dies or hides their faces?"

"No, I once pursued the coin in my youth, and I never left the mountain. I will die here, but not up there."

Solineus shot Morik a smirk. "See? Not everyone dies."

Her smile broadened. "Only the stubborn, but only the stubborn have a chance. Come! Let us eat."

The steps were steep, narrow, uneven, and worn round by rain and thousands of feet over the centuries, but they stood stable despite the patchwork filling cracks and missing chunks. Solineus entered into darkness through the door atop the climb, his eyes adjusting with rapid blinks after days of mountain sun. A hall grew from a dim impression into a distinct place so different from the outside world that It stood narrow with an arched ceiling, maybe a dozen strides across, but a single row of pillars stretched deep into the mountain, strange and disconcerting to the eye like the infinity of standing between two mirrors, but this was a mirror he could step into.

The columns stood seamless with the floor and ceiling, parts of the mountain carved around rather than placed, then chiseled with figures and decorations. The pillar straight in front of him bore a hammer cut into its face, a popular symbol which might represent a fistful of gods in the Pantheon of the Foundations, but the tongs with a smoking ingot clutched in its bite suggested it honored Filinthrôk the Smith, brother and right hand of Rînkodûl, and he who forged the weapons the Foundational Gods wielded during the Age of God Wars.

He glanced at every pillar as they passed, noting the hammers, the sickles, the goat-horns, swords, axe, and fires, but he lacked the expertise to identify to which most gods most of these honored.

Twenty-two pillars down the hall the Seblêsu turned, stepping through a passage Solineus would've strolled straight past without ever noticing, and he glanced back, wondering if, indeed, they hadn't passed several hidden entries. Looking back brought his hand to his chin to rub his whiskers. He peered the way they'd been headed, then back to their entry again; infinity stretched in both directions, an illusion of form or of magic? But his guides were disappearing without giving him time for questions.

He trotted after them, slipping in beside Morik. "That there hall messes with a man's head."

The Kingdomer glanced at him, dead pan eyes. "What do you mean?"

Solineus squinted and puzzled the man; it wasn't a game, Morik didn't know what he spoke of. "It looks normal to you?"

It was Seblêsu who answered: "You've a barbarian's eyes, not the senses of a Kingdomer. Only with direction from Ôls-hûin, the Great Finder, would you see the Hall of Eternity for what it is."

It was Ôls-Hûin who lead the Foundational Gods from the Bellows of Creation to find these mountains, so they might establish the Great Kingdoms of mortal men. This according to the tales Morik told him of the creation of the universe. "What would I see if I were able?"

"This is not for us to say. It is for you to earn, and for Ôls-hûin to bestow, if you are able and he is willing." The priestess stopped and gestured to another near-invisible passage. "Feast. I have matters to attend, but I will return soon to guide you to your quarters."

Solineus bowed. "What're the odds of the Great Finder gifting me with the vision to see?"

She clutched her hands at her waist and smiled. "If you survive the journey to the summit… Well, what isn't possible?" She gave a solemn nod before turning and strolling back the way they came.

Morik said, "Come. It is time we fill our bellies in preparation for your death."

Solineus laughed, a levity he couldn't regret despite the frown on the man's face, and he spoke in Silone. "You are one morose son of a bitch."

The Kingdomer shrugged. "In my experience, the more times I speak a thing true, the less likely it is to happen."

"In that case, my friend, lead me to this meal and pronounce my doom often."

❮❋❋❋❯

After a supper of goat in a mushroom sauce, which threatened to burst his innards, they slept and didn't awaken until the sun careened toward midday. Solineus didn't know what to expect, sitting lonesome in a room made comfortable by a bed and chairs covered in velvet plush, but by the time Morik arrived he welcomed something to do.

They climbed into the outer world to stand beside the lookout tower he'd seen the day before. Morik handed him a walking stick and they strolled at a gentleman's pace. The ascent stood steep for the first several hundred yards, and

Solineus' lungs labored more than he expected by the time they reached the top of the first climb.

Morik opened his canteen. "Practice now. Deep breaths, three swallows, and breathe deep again. The higher we get the more important this will become. The mountain can dry a man to the bone, but drinking too much you might forget to breathe."

"And die."

"Yes."

Solineus drank as he was told, slapped the bung back into its hole. "Lead on."

Morik led him slow and steady, and by early evening they reached the camp known as Nelflûk. Compared to the Temple of Arumbor it was a collection of puny hovels, but the three stone buildings were more than he'd hoped. A handful of pilgrims greeted them, but Morik insisted they didn't waste their breaths on banter. They stood, gazed at the wonder of the rises and falls that were the Dragonspan Mountains across a distance too far to fathom. Then, Morik lead him back down the mountain, where they ate, drank mugs of water, slept, and awoke to climb to Nelflûk again. For six days they did this, but on the seventh eleven porters reappeared with packs filled with supplies.

They climbed to Nelflûk again, and this time they claimed the largest building, built a fire, and shared meals with the men and women who carried the supplies. Morik called these folks Temerêun, something akin to "summit people" when translated. They lived their lives in encampments above the lives of most folks: hunters, explorers, prospectors, miners, a people hardened by their choice of lives, and so they were the finest porters for scaling these heights. They were respected throughout the Eight Kingdoms and seen as outside the normal politics; no kingdom claimed a Temerêun as their own even when they lived within their borders.

A call arose from outside and all eleven porters rose in unison and filed out the door. Morik jabbed him with an elbow and stood, leading him outside. The Temerêun stood in a row staring into the mountains, and he and Morik joined them.

The setting sun illuminated blue skies, white peaks, mottled brown stone mountain faces, and green valleys; harsh and beautiful in the heights falling to plush and hospitable valleys below. The Dragonspans offered a glimpse of the risks, rigors, and rewards of every mortal's life in a single awe-inspiring view. Solineus' breaths came deep and easy, his eyes and thoughts lost in the distant wonders, and so he didn't notice when a lone woman raised her voice in song. A drone which slipped him further into meditative thoughts until he wobbled. He blinked and steadied his feet as one porter, then another, joined in her tune, but he didn't understand the words.

He leaned into Morik's ear. "What are they saying?"

All the Temerêun sang now, eleven voices in harmony despite saying nothing the same. "These are not words; it is known as the Mountain Tongue. The mountain fills their souls, and their voices carry life and inspiration."

Solineus smiled and gazed back to the mountains and the orange sun setting, his muscles mellowing, fingers relaxed at his hips. Morik's voice rose beside him, deep and touched by a melancholy tone, and moments later Solineus joined in the song, though he had no memory of ever singing before. The Mountain Tongue rolled from his lungs to vibrate his tongue. His song was sound without words, emotion without source, wordless and without meaning, and yet somehow, he knew that in the Mountain Tongue his song mattered.

Four

Hollowing Breaths

Do you recall the city of Mâgmermôn?
No, you wouldn't, couldn't, or at least, shouldn't.
It stands in a time lost to all but my mind,
the hind kind biting on the rind,
choking on the marrow while crunching the bone.
Where She stood I stand, a foul and cindered land,
boiled low and smoked high,
the cost of a singular and crucial lie.

—*Tomes of the Touched*

Morning came and they climbed alone from Camp Nelflûk to Camp Ûlf-Hôtindîn, named for two builders who oversaw its construction. The trek was longer but less steep and marked by growing fields of snow; they arrived by midday hale and whole. His lungs felt the strain of the air, but with purposeful and steady strides Solineus figured he'd acquitted himself well enough for a low-lander. The camp consisted of five buildings, all small but sturdy and thick-stoned.

Eight pilgrims greeted them on their arrival, three on their way back down the mountain, but as before, they didn't converse long before Morik had him practicing his breathing and drinking. They descended in time to make Nelflûk well-before nightfall, and they sang at sunset after supping.

Five more days they followed this routine, and on the sixth, the second half of the Temerêun porters joined them, and they claimed a building at the new camp, and they sang at sunset, but this time, from below came the Mountain Tongue of those porters left behind.

Camp Îrginhîn was next, a twin of Nelflûk with three buildings, and the routine was much the same, as they then struck for Camp Zjindinfôk, which was when the journey changed. Every step strained him to the marrow as fatigue crept into his muscles with a weakening ache, and thirst came stronger than before. A coughing fit lightened his head on the climb, and he took a knee to keep from tumbling, to take deep recovering breaths. Snow and ice surrounded them now, not just in patches as before, and Morik handed him spiked straps to attach to his boots for traction. The cold approached the bite of the Treaty Lands, but so far, no fresh snows.

When they reached the lone, tiny building which stood as camp Zjindinfôk, Morik led him straight inside and spoke words over a white boulder sitting in the middle of the room. The stone glowed, and Solineus rushed to its side to find it emanated a pleasant heat; he hugged its girth until sweat beaded on his brow, and it forced him to step away.

They practiced breathing and drinking as the room grew warm enough to remove their gloves, and Solineus didn't have the urge and energy for chatter. All he wanted was to get his ass the hells back down the mountain, but he'd need to climb through clouds to get there.

The descent was a different form of hell, slipping and sliding in sections, but it was a stroll compared to the journey up. Two more days they made the journey light in the packs, but on the next day they loaded supplies; the porters would travel no further, Morik and he were on their own. The weight they carried, with an extra day's food and water, would've been nothing in the valleys far below, but nonetheless it grew heavy on the shoulders at these heights. His thighs and shoulders, hells, every muscle he knew to name and then some, burned under the extra weight, and they toted the supplies for five days before Morik declared they'd stay the night.

The next morning, they didn't climb. They ate, they drank, they breathed, and they rested in the stone's glowing warmth. In six days, he would set forth for the summit as accustomed to these heights as he'd ever get.

Three swallows and breathe, it was fast becoming habit, and he wondered if he might carry it with him back to lower ground. "Who the hells put a shrine so high folks die trying to see it?" Half-humor, half-serious, he didn't expect an answer, and at first, he didn't get one.

Morik stood and warmed his hands as wind howled outside. "Holy scripture says it wasn't always so. The Shrine of

Hîmr was once within reach of all pilgrims, but during the Age of God Wars, they say the mountain rose."

"Hells of a lever to lift a mountain."

Morik smirked. "In those days, in a time the holy name the Black Watered Years… a god of an allied people, the Trickster, brought Markîk the Blessed Fool to the World's Mouth."

While Solineus had picked up on the name Markîk before, one of the gods killed during the God Wars, the story lost him in its words. "Tell me, how would anyone let themselves be fooled by someone named Trickster?"

Morik chortled. "This god's real name has been Forgotten for over five hundred years."

"And this world's mouth?"

"A cavern which drops deep into the world's bowels, so far as to reach magma. We know where it lies, though the lava below has cooled. I've never made the pilgrimage but have heard the tales of those who've lowered into its depths. At this hole in the world, the Trickster drove a spear into the Fool's belly and shoved him into its depths. This Trickster assumed him dead, took his shape, and sought out the Storm-Eye, to deceive and kill him as well. Rînkodûl could not be found, but this false Markîk deceived Hîmr, the Eye's Hammerfall, who commanded the armies of the Foundations. With guile he led Hîmr into an ambush in the mountains, but Hîmr survived and fled into the caves, where he found Sanzumôk and Korhânun to aid in his fight."

Solineus held up his hand. "Hîmr I've heard before, named the Sleeping Dead?"

"Aye, but his proper name is *Eye's Hammerfall.* These three Foundationals battled with ferocity, but were outnumbered, so they fled deeper until all three fought their final battle somewhere in the depths of these mountains."

Solineus knew the man well enough to understand that his squinting eye meant he was in thought. "What more?"

"Heresies... But since you will die soon, I will speak of them."

Solineus breathed deep, took three swallows, and breathed again. "I reckon he wasn't renamed the Sleeping Dead without cause."

"A name you shouldn't have heard. Yes, the Sleeping Dead. The Canon of Helmveline maintains these gods died, but some claim they still live." He leaned against the heating stone, heavy furs guarding him from a burn. "Some sects say these gods fled into an underground river and disappeared... died most of these even agree, but survived say others. They say the Trickster followed, and unable to kill one or all of them, he trapped them for eternity in a rush of lava. Defeated and imprisoned, but alive. The Storm-Eye and the remaining Foundationals never recovered from the loss of their greatest war-leader, and so the enemy subjugated and enslaved us."

Solineus squinted, he missed something. "What's this to do with this mountain?"

"The shrine above is dedicated to Hîmr, and the initial battle was fought here, and when he first fell in ambush, the fighting was so fierce that the world-shaking blows raised Himr's Foundation so high to the sun that its rays burnt away the air. But… others claim when the Trickster trapped Hîmr in lava, that the god used the last of his strength to connect his being with this shrine, to steal the air, to continue to breathe this air, and so stay alive in his tomb of lava. Meditating. Sleeping. Waiting to be freed."

"The Sleeping Dead."

"Yes. A story for a child! But many believe some version of the tale."

"The Trickster, a god of the Hokandite?"

Morik stepped from the boulder with a shrug. "No one knows, but many assume it so."

"And if the air above is stolen still…" The implications furrowed his brow. "They believe he's alive and still connected to the shrine; he wasn't banished from the world."

Morik's gaze fell heavy on him, his eyes dark with shadow from the boulder's glow. "You are quick, for a barbarian. They are fools, but fools with powerful ideas are the most dangerous sort."

Solineus stood and moseyed to the boulder's side. "What would these people think of a foreigner claiming the Himr's coin?"

Morik snorted, tugged his beard. "I don't rightly know. Worry about it after you don't die, which you will."

I won't be some hero to anyone but the Helmveline, maybe not all of them. "Well, hells. Life'd be a bore without a bunch of people wanting me dead."

"Nobody cares. Not yet." Morik sat, then stretched out in his bed of heavy furs. "If the weather holds, you will climb and die soon enough."

{❄❄❄}

When the three priests arrived, Solineus realized his time to climb neared without counting the days. The next morning the five of them ate breakfast and stepped into a blinding world dominated by the sun above, and the priests held hands, turning back to back in a sort of triangle. A droning prayer arose in unison and their eyes scanned the horizon up and down in every direction, as if able to see through the mountain upon which they stood, and all those around. The prayerful drone concluded, and a priestess declared:

"Not today." And the devout filed back into the building.

Solineus stared at Morik. "What the hells was that?"

The Kingdomer shrugged and stepped back into the building without a word; Solineus followed with a grumble. No more than a candle later he got his answer. Buffeting winds howled and brought snow enough to bury a man standing if it weren't wiped from the mountain by the same winds which carried the flakes to Zjindinfôk in the first place. The snows relented within candles, but the wind remained for three days, so stiff it might remove a man from the mountain side with a gust. So, they ate and drank and breathed in damned near silence, as the three priests spoke nary a word, and Morik pinned his mouth shut.

The fifth morning after the priests arrived, they awoke to sunshine and a quiet sky, and the trio prayed. When they stopped, the woman pronounced: "Today."

Morik strapped a light pack to his back and handed him five canteens of water. "Drink slow, you don't want to swallow the hot rocks keeping the water from freezing."

"What's it matter if I'm going to die anyhow?"

"Because they won't kill you… it'll just hurt like a shit-devil until you squat it out."

It made an ugly sort of sense. With a hot rock in his mittens and boots, freezing to death wasn't the issue he'd feared, and no doubt eating one would be unpleasant without the kindness of killing him. Solineus smirked. "I see. Personal experience?"

"There've been drunken wagers… not my own, mind, but suffice to say I never heard of no man swallowing one twice." Morik slapped his back with a bear hug. "Die peacefully, my friend."

Solineus shrugged the grasp away. "Death isn't for me." A muted clap came from his mittens as he slapped them together, then he hit the latch on the Twins and they fell to his hips. "Just in case it ain't the air, and there's something up there wanting to eat me." He tested his cleated feet, and Morik handed him two climbing sticks, sturdy and tipped with steel to penetrate snow and ice. The sky was a peculiar, dark blue so high in the sky.

He turned to face the climb as the priests broke into a chanting prayer, and he strode forward. Slow. Steady. Breathing. *Steady heart, steady steps. Half a horizon's climb, and it's down I go.*

After a hundred strides he turned to look back, his breath already thin. Wisps of cloud raced by and he raised a hand in salute. Soon after, he rounded a corner, a pillar of jagged ice, and wouldn't see a living soul again until his return. The ascent here was tame compared to previous locations, and there were no crevasses to bridge, thank the gods, so he kept his head down and eyes focused on the packed snow in front of him.

The first landmark he reached was a cliff which bore the name Râkêr's Rope, for the man who first scaled its height three hundred years earlier. He was also one of the first to die striving for the peak. A thick, frozen stretch of rope dangled from the slope's top to a steel spike driven into the ground at the base, but in fact it was several ropes, none the original. Solineus pulled a fresh rope from his pack and tied it to the stake before taking hold of the old rope and climbing higher.

Cleats sinking into snow and rope in hand made the climb less brutal than he'd expected, and once at the top he tied off his new rope, a salute to the original, and a boon to future climbers. Two candles into the climb by this time, he sat and stared at the sky while breathing and drinking, taking a few bites of jerked goat. He groaned to his feet and trudged onward along a slender ridge with falls to either side no man without wings would survive, but with his eyes trained tight to the snow in front of him, and counting to one hundred over and over to test his mental acuity, he managed to ignore the doom at either hand until he reached a flat stretch on the other side.

Looking back, he imagined that this narrow stretch of ice was a place many climbers met their end with heavy winds. More water. More breathing. And as he took his first stride to round a bend, he stopped. A mound of ice and snow sat frozen to a stone wall, too human in shape to ignore. He swiped at the form, and a fur collar appeared from beneath falling snow. A climber, no doubt, but with an odd tilt to his head.

He drew a Twin, and regret struck him with a wave of nausea as the sword's voice wormed into his consciousness. He wobbled, hilt clacking the icy ground to stabilize himself. "Easy, Sister." Deep breaths, and the voice relented, the whispers soft and gentle. He blinked in a flurry as he recovered and brought the Latcu edge to bear against the ice, shaving layers, careful not to remove parts of the dead man. The corpse's head was well-preserved and tilted with an unnatural lean; his throat was cut to damned near removing his head. "Nothing ate you, at least." He sucked a deep breath and drank, recalling the priestess' words about competition in the quest for Hîmr's Coin. If one had killed the other, the next question was what ended the murderer's climb.

He sheathed the Sister, nabbed his walking stick and stood, taking a few moments to breathe. A third of the way to the summit, he guessed. *Eyes ahead, steady steps and breaths.*

Around the next bend he found a field of jagged snow just as Morik had said he would, a slope known as Yôgul's Fall. Folks didn't so much die here, as they turned back. Steep and slick and without a rope, its quick rise in altitude was what had turned the priestess for home, sending her to the Temple of Arumbor to serve the mountain and its shrine as Lady of the Mountain.

The climb was twenty paces forward, pick and stick, with slides ten paces back if you messed up. His lungs and muscles burned, and his tongue cursed every time he fell back. He slammed a spiked toe into the ice and pulled the Twins. The blades sunk easy into the ice and he pulled himself up with the help of his cleated boots. So pleased with himself he forgot to breathe; his head spun and the whispers of the Twins wrenched his wits back into his head.

Deep breaths. And he didn't slip another step on this section of climb.

Atop Yôgul's Fall sat a flat ledge, and here he again took a break for water and a few bites of meat, before moving on. He glanced at the world from these heights and mused it might be beautiful if the mountain weren't trying to kill him. *Maybe once resettled in the valleys, and I forget the aches and swimming head, I'll appreciate the grandeur.*

The path was smooth with snow and ice, and broader than he was tall, and even if he fell from a side, he doubted it'd kill him outright. Death would instead be slow as he struggled to climb back. Muscles tingled and ached, and his count to one hundred skipped numbers here and there, or fell back to start again. Catching himself, he'd kneel and breathe, drink. And breathe. And it wasn't long before he saw the summit ahead.

But it was still a long time away. Or a short time, if he walked in a green valley. But here, a couple hundred strides of climb felt as an eternity, and might be just that if he failed; a precipice sat at the bottom of the climb, and its fall held a crushing end several hundred feet below. *Steady steps and steady breaths,* and a candle later his head poked over the crown of the world, and his breath near disappeared. If not from the sun burning the air away at these heights, if not from a god stealing the air, then from what he saw: The world of snow and ice turned ruddy stone brown and gray, barren of life or chill, but the plateau lay spotted by the dead.

The nearest fur-clad corpse lay no more than twenty paces away, frozen in an eternal crawl toward a rise of black obsidian, maybe five feet high, which resembled a skinny volcano with what he suspected was a hollow crater on top. He counted the bodies but stopped at thirty; how many died didn't matter. Every one of them faced the shrine, each failing to scratch and claw their way to the treasure and the renown it would bring.

He spiked his boots into the ice and peered over the edge, getting as comfortable as he could to study the scene.

None of them looked eaten on, at least from this vantage, despite seeing bones, but this only eliminated normal critters; there were things in the world which fed on other than flesh and blood… or, their blood could be drained. There was no way to know anything for certain, and if a creature did this, odds on it stared at him now.

His eyes discerned nothing that might be a predator.

Dead air? If so, it was more than altitude, because his head was above the plateau's plain and he breathed well enough. *How many of those dead in front of me stood here, thinking, and still they died?*

Deep breaths. Clear thoughts.

And a puff of air tickled his face. Dead calm, except for that single puff; there was never not a wind, until now. He raised his fur clad mitten and watched as the hairs leaned, then stopped. So soft, as if he blew on them from a foot away. Flickers later they reversed, leaning back toward the shrine, and he turned his head. The puff hit his face from the other direction. A gentle breeze on a mountain whose winds threatened to carry him from its face a hundred times. A gods-cursed place at the top of the world; no, there needn't be some monster here to bare his bones to the winds and sun.

Bones. The bodies should never thaw, how are there bones? And no snow. The mountain height slowed his brain.

He reached for the bare ground with a fur-clad hand and lay it there. Flickers later his hand warmed through the mitten. "I'll be damned." He slipped his hand free, bare skin to the rock, but it wasn't just the stone which warmed his fingers. The air was pleasant, warmer than anything felt since trekking from Shuntiskâ.

He slipped the mitten back on and stared. Any man would welcome this reprieve after the climb to get here, but for the dead littering the area. Death by warm breeze, no doubt, it could get worse than that.

A candle later he stared still at the macabre scene, chewing on spiced goat and breathing. Nothing moved, nothing changed, just the breeze back and forth across his exposed skin. *I didn't come so far to turn back.* But he didn't come so far to die, either.

He stuffed his meal back in its pouch and huffed, making the same godsdamned determination he guessed many of the dead before him had made: There was no way to know how to defeat the danger he faced without experiencing it.

He crept forward, sticking his face into the incoming breeze.

Warmth.

Before air surged into his chest. His lungs felt near to bursting and his cheeks filled. He coughed with the rush of air, head spinning. Lost his footing. Slid.

Scrambling for a grip the ice defied his clutching fingers and cleats alike, and he rolled onto his back, hammering spiked heels. He slowed, creeping toward the sheer cliff at the end; if he lifted a heel, he might never slow himself again. He drew the Twins with caution, their voices subdued as if to not overwhelm his mind, and he slipped their tips into the ice. Heels and blades were enough to stop him, but he was three feet from his toes dangling. The Twins cut the ice too easy, the climbing sticks were worthless here, dangling from his wrists, and his pick-axe was at the top of the climb.

A deep breath before lifting his left foot, and he could feel the spike of his right heel shift. He slammed his boot, tested its grip, and shoved back. Step by step back up the slide until he felt secure enough to roll over and put his toes spikes to use. Only on reaching the top a second time did he stop to consider what the hells happened.

A te-xe? A wind forced into my lungs, but not hitting my skin. An air elemental might explain the rush of air into his lungs, but he saw nothing of a creature. *How the hells would I know if a being of air is able to be seen?* An insubstantial and invisible enemy was something he couldn't defeat with a sword; he couldn't be certain it was even there. Reaching the coin wouldn't be a fight, it'd be a struggle.

Thinking did him no good; there was one direction, and that was forward. Three deep breaths, a drink, and more deep breaths. He waited for the breeze to hit his face, held his breath, and clawed his way onto bare rock. The surge struck, and he clutched his nose to keep the air from penetrating, and he dashed toward the shrine.

The breeze ended.

Reversed.

And breath sucked from his lungs.

No stopping it. He gasped and flopped to the ground,

his eyeballs dried and swelling in their sockets. Against reason he drew the Twins, their voices surging within his mind, terrified for his life without an enemy to battle. He flailed as a fish tossed ashore, knees and elbows lumbering as a wounded bear toward the shrine, Latcu blades notching the stone where they struck.

Tranquility. And the puff of breeze returned. His nose and throat burned with assailing air, and he tucked his face into an elbow, biting his lips to keep them closed. He scrambled to his feet and dashed, striking the obsidian shrine with his shoulder as the air was ripping from his lungs. He glanced to the body of a woman beside him; they'd both gotten this far, so close. He sheathed the Brother and buried his face in his elbow, clenching his eyes shut, waiting for the air to return. Still air. The rush.

Nausea and pain, but he clenched his lips and stood, throwing his hand to the top of the shrine. Something rattled beneath his fingers, but his eyes wouldn't open. He shrugged his mitten off and grabbed a warm disc of metal.

The coin.

It was his.

But his breath was not.

Air ripped from his lungs and he collapsed to his back, staring at a dark blue sky that went black.

Vision drifted to blue and gray, swirling, the familiar worms of the Lady's world crawling beneath his skin with the warm waves. He breathed, but there was pain, and speaking spun his mind, and the words came out all wrong. "You are… where… I'm…"

Her voice came from everywhere and nowhere. "Hush, love. Don't waste your breath. Think, don't speak."

Three breaths, deep. Three deep breaths. Remember to breathe. "I'm dead."

"Not quite, and I'd prefer you didn't. I've grown fond of you." The Lady faded into existence by his side, her body stretched down the length of his, her lips close, her breath warm on his cheek. "Relax." And her lips covered his.

Warmth. Sensuality. Perfect calm. And he breathed with her breaths instead of the mountain's puffs, the scent and taste of lilac on his tongue and breath. He breathed through her lips, into his lungs, then back into hers in a strange unison, bringing to his mind the push and pull of working a two-man saw. The union of circular breathing felt unnatural at first, but he grew accustomed to the back and forth, and his lips molded with hers.

Her thoughts entered his head: *Five more breaths and I release you. Hold my breath and walk, reach the clean air, I may not be able to save you a second time.*

He gazed into her consuming eyes, his lips shaping hers into a smile. *I won't need a second time.*

The Sister murmured in one hand, and the other clutched the coin, as his eyes flicked open. He stood with full lungs and the lilac scent of the Lady still in his nostrils, and fought the urge to run. The mountain's puff buffeted his face, and on departing pulled at his lips and nostrils, but the Lady's air wouldn't leave his lungs. Still, it was a long time to hold a breath while walking slow.

He stuffed the coin in a pouch, sheathed the Sister, and walked with calm and confidence until he reached the edge of the plateau. He dropped to his knees then lay flat, sticking his head out into the snow before exhaling with a rush. And he grinned as frozen air filled his lungs.

Exhausted, muscles burning, and his head spinning, he doubted he'd survive the climb down to the next ledge, let alone beyond. He reached into his pack and pulled out a heavy fur and wrapped his face and head, tucking the remainder under his head for a pillow. A short rest.

There wasn't a choice. No better one, anyhow.

And so he curled there, breathing deep of frigid air filtered through fur, while the rest of his body lay on bare stone, warm as if camped in a low-land valley.

Five

Share and Share

Whisker twitch scenting the wind,
the Hunter's tongue tasting dirt—
Oh! the flirt, the hurt, the nonsensical Blurt!
Ha-ha-ha! Strike the laughter! No!
Scratch the strike!
A proof of humor is a proof of mortality.
A proof of sanity in the inanity.
I digress into the egress.
The predator eats the bunny,
and the artist swipes swaths with
whisker brush. So noble, to die for another's art.
Ha-ha!

—*Tomes of the Touched*

Solineus stumbled into Camp Zjindinfôk by the light of the moon and leaned on the entrance to the single building to find it barred. His shoulders ached, his body stiff at every joint. He rapped the wooden door with a knee thrice, and it opened to reveal a familiar and hairy face.

"Are you a ghost?"

"I reckon a ghost wouldn't be this godsdamned cold and tired."

Morik slipped beneath his arm and helped him to a seat beside the glowing stone as Solineus glanced around: The priests were gone. "They left early?"

"You arrived late, and they assumed you dead."

Solineus unwrapped his right hand, its mitten still sitting atop the mountain, and warmed it on the stone as the man stared at him. "What?"

"What? What do you mean, what? The coin, did you get it?"

Solineus wiggled the stiff from his fingers and reached into a pocket. "Too godsdamned big to be a coin, but I found something."

Brilliant gold in color, but he suspected it was an alloy or some such. It was so big his fingers needed to stretch to palm the thing by its edges. A disc, half a finger thick, imprinted with animals and characters he didn't understand.

"The Five Earls be one—"Morik stroked his beard"—you did it."

Solineus stared at the thing; no doubt it was valuable, but no doubt in his mind it wasn't worth the lives scattered across the mountain's slopes. But he'd been wrong before. "If'n you say so." He proffered the coin, and Morik took it with tentative fingers.

The Kingdomer tumbled it from hand to hand. "No idea what it says, though the lightning and war-hammer refer to Hîmr." He buffed the coin against his fur-clad leg and held the thing to the light of the stone; a translucent purple shown, shaped as a flower, with the illusion of being deeper in the metal than the disc was thick. "The metal is Timôu, like gold but so much more. It weighs half a brick… worth a fortune even without its provenance."

"So, men would kill for it?"

"Would men kill for it?" Morik laughed and handed it back to him. "Aye. You hold it safe with them swords. And might I suggest, again, a shield?"

Solineus grinned. "I'll consider it."

"What was it like? At the summit."

Solineus took three breaths and drank, then breathed some more. "Something's up there… maybe. It's a warm plateau at the very peak, not a flake of snow, and this breeze is light on the face… it forces its way into your lungs like a gale til you damned near explode, then it takes every bit of your breath, trying to suck your eyes from your head."

Morik cocked his head. "Nothing I've heard of."

"A powerful *te-xe* is my only thought."

"An elemental of air? They aren't aggressive, so I've heard."

"Hells if I know, friend. But no, it didn't seem to be trying to kill me, or it damned well would've. The force… it just was. We don't mean to kill every bug we step on, but we still do… that's how it felt. I was caught in its nature, not its will."

"Or you'd be dead."

"I'd be dead." He didn't mention the Lady of the blue universe saving him. One crazy tale at a time. "I got lucky not dying the first time the air struck, so I covered my face, pinched my nose, and still damned near died. I wouldn't try it again."

Morik grinned. "I wouldn't try it a first time. When you are able, we should move down the mountain."

"Eat, warm these bones… the sun rises I want off this godsdamned mountain fast as I can… without rolling or plummeting to the bottom."

Morik laughed and put a kettle atop the boulder. "Tea with a sniff of whiskey… just a drop, to celebrate."

{❋❋❋}

They reached Camp Îrginhîn a couple candles after sunrise, and though a dozen pilgrims resided in the buildings, Morik cautioned not to mention Himr's coin. It was the first time Solineus saw Morik nervous around another Kingdomer, whether of Helmveline or more distant kingdom. His had been a fool's question: would a man kill for this coin. He scoffed at himself. The unanswerable question was how many and who were they?

By midday they reached Ûlf-Hôtindîn, and here they decided to rest and spend the night. They ate with a handful of pilgrims and their Temerêun porters and sang in the mountain tongue before bedding for the night. Come morning they hiked to Nelflûk, with a quick rest before heading to the Temple of Arumbor.

A droning voice rose from the watchtower as they descended the final horizon; the secret of the coin wouldn't survive much longer.

Seblêsu, Lady of the Mountain, swept toward them with hasty strides and met them three hundred paces outside the temple grounds. Her hands rubbed together, her eyes wide with curiosity. "You have the coin?"

"I do."

She exhaled with a whistle and a smile. "My prayers suggested it was so, but it was too much to believe after the priests returned." She turned her back to them and raised her arms. "Tonight, is the feast of Himr! The coin has arrived!"

Stunned faces on those close enough to discern, and total silence as folks turned to stare, the words taking flickers to soak in. Then, cheers rang, echoing across the valley, and other voices sang in the Mountain Tongue. Two dozen men and women charged him, and if not for their smiles, he would've drawn the Twins. They circled him, hugging him in turns, thanking him for his feat.

Seblêsu strolled toward the tower which held stairs descending into the temple proper. "Prepare the feast of Himr!"

Solineus smiled and hugged every comer, stumbling as they pressed tight, but the coin rested deep inside layers of heavy cloaks where no hand would reach without him knowing. Surrounded by bodies and praise they made their way to the temple slower than he'd covered some sections of the climb.

He bathed in steaming waters with Morik and several Helmveline men standing guard at the door. Already, folks had tried stealing his clothes, but not to find the coin. Folks desired a piece of history, artifacts of the man who conquered the mountain, relics to pass down to generations to come… or to sell for a fortune, if Morik spoke true.

More disturbing? How much a vial of his blood might be worth.

But hot water melted these concerns and turned his spirit to musings of Lelishen slipping into the water with him, and he dozed, imagining it so. When his eyes fluttered open the water no longer steamed, and his skin was wrinkled like an old and soggy potato. He stretched the kink in his neck and rose, throwing on fresh undergarments, blue and gold silk robes (where the coin now rested in an interior pocket), and the Twins on his back. Boots of mottled leather, nothing he'd dare wear outside in the frigid cold, slipped onto his feet with a supple hug and he wiggled his toes. He cinched his silken belt with satisfaction. Being an instant legend had its perks.

He eased to the door and opened it a crack. Morik stood the watch still, but from the looks of his hair and garb, he too had seen a tub of water.

"You smell better."

Solineus laughed. "Who the hells could smell a thing in that cold?"

"True enough. Come, the eating waits on us."

They walked the hall surrounded by warriors of the Helmveline, passing through the halls in rigid order; their shields were on their backs, and their hands didn't stray to their weapons, but the march bore the hallmark of nerves with eyes checking every hall and balcony.

"I'd like to get a message to Kinesee soon as possible."

"This must wait until we reach Molikîn. Every pigeon has been sent with word of the coin."

Solineus squinted, uncertain if he appreciated the whole of the Eight Kingdoms marking him as a hero and target so soon. "How safe are we?"

"A boy came to us with a whisper of trouble, claiming he overheard men wanting to take the coin, but wanting and trying are two different things. Still, we'll leave for Molikîn come morning. No coincidence the Ironwing sent with you men who can fight."

They stepped into the mountain air to the sound of cheers, but the sun blinded him; when his eyes recovered an uncomfortable smile spread. Hundreds of people, common folks from their gear, raised their hands and sang to him.

"Shits. How long was I in that bath?"

"Word travels fast, and there are villages and mines not so far from here."

Solineus waved to the crowd, but Morik knocked his hand down. "Don't make yourself a clearer target than you already are. This range, a crossbowman might put a bolt in your eye."

"Poor way to get the coin."

"Good way to protest a foreigner's intrusion."

The train of warriors passed through a broad door into the temple without the twang of a tensioned string, and within a hundred paces they entered a wide hall teeming with priests and servants and carts filled with food and drink. A dozen circular tables, hollowed in the middle for servants, with a dozen chairs each, were spaced between pillars thirty feet high. A priest in green robes trotted to them, bowed, then led them to the Seblêsu's table. Solineus remove the Twins and hung them from the back of his chair before taking a seat by her side. Morik and men of Helmveline filled out the table while others stood watch nearby.

The commotion of the hall settled from a roar to a buzz and everyone sat. The Seblêsu stood, taking a goblet of liquor in her hand and raising it high. Everyone stood, and Solineus tried to follow suit, but Morik held his shoulder down, and shot him a quick nod.

"Tonight, we honor Solineus Mikjehemlut of the Clan Emudar, favored of Hîmr the Hammerfall, the fallen hand of the Storm-Eye. Solineus! He who has retrieved the coin of Hîmr, returning it to its people in service to the Kingdom of Helmveline. A great debt we owe this man! Not solely for bringing us the coin, but for saving so many who would otherwise have died in its pursuit. To Solineus, the Survivor of Hîmr's Breath!"

She snatched the knife from the table and tapped the goblet's rim, and a piercing chime echoed through the room. A hundred rings joined the din, and Solineus struggled to smile through the racket. When she stopped the echo faded, and only when silent did she sit. The flicker she settled into her seat, the table was beset by servants doling out food and drink. Goat meat, jellies, four varieties of berry, and a handful of different breads, but the delicacies clamored for were trout eggs in a spiced honey and pheasant in elderberry sauce. Solineus tried everything with a smile but ate bread the most. A spice he didn't have a name for permeated every course and gave his tongue a curl; when he learned the name later, he'd be sure to avoid it.

The spice was bad enough, getting evil looks from Morik whenever he reached for wine or beer turned him peevish, but it was clear that not a single man of Helmveline took part in the drinking. Morik had understated the threat, or the man was more cautious than imagined.

The evening moved on, and as cakes covered in a sweet, purple sauce were served, the drone of the Mountain Song came from outside the temple. Sundown. Hundreds of voices. He cocked his head, listening to the unusual beauty of so many voices singing different things.

He put his fork to the cake and stuffed a bite into mouth. He had no idea what he ate but regretted all the bread from earlier. "This is spectacular."

Seblêsu smiled. "Elderberry-rhubarb, generously sweetened. A treat from the Kingdom of Ôkô." She stared at him as he ate, awkward seeing as she'd ignored him since her speech. "Might I make a rub of the coin?"

Solineus stopped in mid-chew, swallowed. "What's a rub?"

"I place thin vellum over the coin's faces and rub it with charcoal, creating a drawing of it, so to speak. You'll be wanting rubs anyhow, to deliver to all the kingdoms for study."

Solineus tapped his fork on what was sadly his first and only glass of wine and glanced to Morik.

The Kingdomer shrugged. "Proper enough. So long as it doesn't leave this table."

Solineus nodded to the priestess. "I'd appreciate one of these rubs… seeing as I won't get to keep the thing."

"Of course." She smiled, snapping her fingers, and a young man trotted to her side. "Ten sheets of vellum and charcoal."

The young priest twined his fingers in front of him and bowed with his knees pressed tight.

Solineus took another bite, but the priestess seemed determined to make sure he didn't enjoy his dessert. "The summit… what did you find."

He paused, swallowed, then stuffed the remainder of the cake in his mouth before relaying the tale. She nodded as he covered as many details as he could recall. All the while, she enjoyed her own dessert with annoying leisure, and when he finished his story, she pried further.

"So, pilgrims could visit the summit in safety? View it, so long as they don't try to breathe the air?"

"Yes. Some would die on the journey, but many would not."

"This is wonderful news! Priests from across the Foundations will be overjoyed to know this truth, to be able to come and offer prayers. A pity you left a mitten behind."

The brow over his left eye cocked. "What's that got to do with anything?"

She grimaced. "Pilgrims will die trying to reach the artifact."

Solineus groaned. "Bow fishing, an arrow with a string. Get the damned thing back before some idiot dies."

A smile and nod. "You might be right. I will consider this. There you are!"

Solineus looked up with a start; the priest stood beside her with an armful of vellum and square sticks of charcoal in his hand. The priestess stood as he lay them on the table.

"May I see the coin?"

"May I have more cake?"

She chortled. "Of course." With a snap of her fingers the priest darted toward a dessert cart, and when the plate of cake rested in front of him, he reached into his robes and brought forth the coin.

The room hushed, and she held it with reverential care, a soft touch as if it was fine crystal rather than a disc of metal that'd survived hundreds of years atop a mountain. She held it high, the fires of the room illuminating the purple flower in its golden sheen, before laying it on the table. She stared, a tear in her eye, as if seeing a lover long thought lost.

Solineus was just happy to have his cake.

She traced a finger along its edge, a deep breath sliding from her chest. "I said I was always an optimist, but I wonder… Seeing it now, I realize I never expected to witness this day, let alone be honored to touch this holy relic." She covered the coin and rubbed, creating a perfect but duller copy. She picked it up, examined its edges. "It is good there's no writing here, that'd make this more difficult." And she flipped the coin to its back and rubbed so that the sheet held copies of each side.

Ten times he watched this ritual, long enough to finish three slices of cake, and each time he resisted the urge to lick the plate. She rolled each vellum and tied them with a thin strand of silvery metal and handed him a copy.

"This one is yours. These others you should bear with you to the Ironwing."

Morik stood and bowed. "My gratitude, Seblêsu." He collected the scrolls and piled them in front of him.

"I should wonder, Solineus... Morik... if you would deign allow people to pass the table and look upon Hîmr's Coin? It is a singular chance in people's lifetimes."

Morik nodded, so Solineus said, "It'd give me time to build hunger for a final piece of cake."

She smiled and bowed. "Thank you. I should deliver this copy to our library, but I will return with swift feet."

Solineus stood and bowed. "Thank you for your hospitality."

The priestess departed with a handful of priests in her wake, and word whispered rumor-quick through the room, and a long line ensued. Solineus scooted from the table and stood, slinging the Twins over his shoulders as he stood to get out of the way of folks. But this was impossible, as he was almost the equal attraction of the coin: the foreigner with Ikoruv hilted Latcu blades, Solineus, the Survivor of Hîmr's Breath.

An odd title, and he decided to ask her about it when she returned.

The Helmveline allowed curious eyes to creep close but swatted away every finger that floated too close to the violet bloom of the golden coin. The line went on and on, people filing in from outside, until his legs grew tired of standing. He leaned on a table, covered a yawn as he nodded to passersby.

The first scream turned the room to statues. Solineus stood straight, craning his neck to look over every man in the room. Men in golden masks, axes and hammers in hand, and no way to grasp their numbers.

The statues turned to a herd of frightened goats before he could say a word, and he was jostled and carried with the flow of fleeing bodies. The Twins flashed from their sheaths with a flurry of whispers and he shoved his way toward the coin. Helmveline warriors drew weapons, but the swarm in flight banged and knocked them around; still, they formed a horseshoe facing the oncoming men in gold.

Solineus edged between bodies to reach the oncoming fray, but stopped; a straight attack made no sense when they had ample chance to… He turned and locked eyes with a man approaching the coin's table. The bastard looked away, but only to slam a dagger up and under a Helmveliner's ribs.

Solineus roared and shoved two people in his path, and as the man's hand reached for the coin the Brother hissed and slashed; the man's arm rested sanguine on the table a foot from its goal, but Solineus was still a branch awash in a stream of people carrying him from the treasure.

He shoved from a man and lunged, tripped by another's foot, and he careened into the table's edge. The table squawked across the floor with his impact and he hit the floor hard enough to ring his ears; in flickers the table toppled and flipped in the chaos, the coin striking the floor fingers from his reach, rolling a foot before kicked.

"Shittin' me?"

He turned the edges of the Twins to the stone floor, to keep from taking off innocent ankles, and scrambled after the traveling disc. Kicked once, twice, and a third time, he figured the good news was most folks didn't have a clue where the thing'd gone.

Feet and shins ricocheted from his hips, ribs, and head, and he tripped at least three people in his pursuit. The coin spun on its edge as if a mystical force refused to let it fall, and he strove to his feet, stumble-running while trying not to kill anyone with the swords in his hands. A woman fell in front of him, and tried to jump, but someone shoved him from behind, and his toe clipped the woman's shoulder. The Twins clattered as splayed to hands and knees, but the coin was only feet away. He dove, and a kneed caught him in the head.

Sister's pommel struck the coin and sent it lurching away, fallen and sliding near the far wall. A young girl picked up the coin, a child no more than seven. He rose to his, sheathing the Sister, and making his way to the child with deep brown eyes and a look of awe on her face. In all the room, he figured he and this girl were the only two who knew where the coin had gotten to.

He kneeled when reaching her and fought for a sincere smile.

He stared. She stared. He didn't have the slightest idea what to say. She could run, scream, hit him…

Instead she held out the coin. "Here you go."

He took the coin and laughed, taken aback by this child's innocence, returning a thing so many would kill for. "Thank you. I owe you one."

He turned to the rattle of combat behind him. Much of the hall stood cleared, but in its middle men fought and died. He reached to stuff the coin in the pocket of his robes and was halfway to drawing Sister… The coin was light. He backed to the wall, pressing the child to his side, and brought forth the coin. As he remembered: the illusory depth of the violet flower, the war-hammer and lightning symbol… But when he turned it over the back-side was gone. He sank against the wall as if someone'd dropped an anchor down his gullet. "Son of a shit…" He glanced at the child, embarrassed by his language, but realized she wouldn't understand Silone anyhow." He held it up for the girl. "It was like this?"

She nodded and he scanned the floor. Nothing. He'd seen the damned thing hit the floor, roll, kicked and kicked again, and he'd never seen it come apart. He leaned in and stared. Where the piece was missing was reamed to twist in and out, so precise he'd never noticed where the two pieces joined. *Who would know… Seblêsu?* The woman flipped and rubbed the coin numerous times— "Morik!" The Kingdomer stood behind his men, commanding them to victory, but his ax too was bloodied. Solineus slipped the coin in his robes and ran to his side, yanked his shoulder. "Morik! Seblêsu has half of Hîmr's coin."

The man's fighting gaze turned on him. "What the Five Earls you talking about?"

He held the coin in front of his face. "She has half the godsdamned coin."

Morik stared, turned his gaze back to the fighting. The Helmveliners were reinforced by priests and pushing the gold-masks back. "What'd she want with half the blessed coin?"

"Hells if I know nor hells if I care, she has it. Where the hells would she go?"

The fighting pushed away, and Morik led him the way the priestess exited. The hall past the door went two directions. "The Eight Ways."

"What the hells is that?"

"Damned near every temple, fortress, city, or village with an underground has an Eight Ways… A place with eight tunnels, several of which lead far away and outside."

"Escape routes."

A young priest trotted down the hall and Morik stepped in his path, hand clutching his collar. "The Eight Ways, take us there."

"Excuse me?" The man swiped at Morik's grip, but the gesture was futile and earned him a good shake.

"Take me to the Eight Ways *now* or I'll happily assume you're in cahoots with the one who stole Himr's Coin."

The priest blanched. "This way." He turned and jogged the way he'd come, Morik right on his heels.

"Faster, priest!"

And they ran, turning through a dozen twists and turns until they exited the hewn halls for natural caves. The priest snagged a torch from a sconce and it lit with a prayer. From here they moved slower, but the journey was short.

They halted in cavern no more than fifty strides across, but a multitude of holes in the mountain led from the chamber.

Morik said, "I count seven, where's eight?"

The priest pointed up; the tunnel was difficult to see in poor light.

Solineus pointed to this raised cave. "Does it lead outside?"

"Yes. Five of them do, the other three will circle you for horizons before a dead-end."

Five choices, and even if they chose the right one, the odds of catching her were slim. "Way I see it… She'd either take that their high tunnel hoping we miss it, or it'd be the last one she'd take because it's the obvious choice for just that reason."

Morik took the torch from the lad. "Sounds like fifty-fifty to me, which is better than one-in-four. Let's climb."

They scaled chiseled steps and Solineus hunched to see if he could spot prints in dust. Nothing. No dust at all. "Damn it, no sign."

"They aren't fools; they keep all the tunnels swept and clean. Come, we're burning time."

The natural cavern twisted and turned, but after a thousand strides turned to hewn stone again. The cut was rough, squared and braced with heavy timbers, and cut a straight line with a mild descent; they fought the urge to run, not knowing how far the tunnel stretched, but jogged for sections. Time was a mystery, but he reckoned they'd been in the cave a candle when a cold wind hit their faces, and within wicks they stepped into a snowy night, flakes melting in the torches flame as they fell from the sky.

They kneeled, the torch's dancing light illuminating prints half-filled by the fresh dusting of snow. Several sets of prints, but most important, hooves created the trail leading west. Morik snorted. "Her lead isn't huge, if she camps for the night…"

Solineus stood, glancing at his silk robes, and oh so soft boots that'd leave his toes black in the frozen mountains. Boots, no doubt, which the priestess had provided for his comfort. "She's gone. By the time we threw our gear together… we'd be leaving in the morning. Catching her would be a prayer, and we still have most of the coin."

"We do at that. But I don't like losing."

"Neither do I. But it was a battle, not the war. We take the coin to the Ironwing, figure out where's she's gone to... then, we go take our godsdamned coin back."

Morik stomped and turned. "What is this we?"

"You wouldn't want me to win the war by myself, would you?" He grinned. "I mean, after all, I defeated the mountain without you."

Morik snorted and turned back into the cave. "Didn't."

Solineus followed. "I didn't see you up there, did I miss you hiding somewhere?"

The Kingdomer grunted. "You would've died... The priestess and coin are your trouble, not mine. I've got a wife and mountain to return to."

"Sure you do. Of course."

Their shadows danced on the walls, ceiling, and floor, and their footfalls fell in time with the echo of dripping water. After a hundred strides: "Forge fires take you."

Solineus grinned but hid his face in shadows. "I knew you'd see it my way."

Six

The Weight of Golden Feathers

See to sea? Lie in sky? Steal to feel? Flap to clap?
Emulsion of lies and truths into bitter recipe,
the slop, the screed, the whistling reed,
the done for no reason deed.
Struggling to crawl to flutter to fall.
Egg to worm, worm to butterfly, butterfly to dust,
dust to make me sneeze.
No matter the tale you begin to tell,
the end comes back to me.

—*Tomes of the Touched*

The streets of Molikîn bustled with a swarm of Helmveliners, their path through the streets so crowded that Solineus' warrior escorts strode with shields formed in a wedge to shove well-wishers and celebrants from their path. A far cry from the subdued tranquility of his first arrival.

Men and women waved long silver poles with streaming banners, fashioned from glistening golden feathers of a multitude of hues, and every man, woman, and child wore bright silks and linens. His arrival was a celebration, and the joyous faces cut a deep emotional swath; he'd been through so much pain and hardship, seen so many folks die that awkward tears swelled his eyes. He didn't let a one fall, and he smiled with twitching lips.

Morik elbowed him and spoked in Silone. "Wave, clap… walking like the dead will make them think you don't appreciate your success."

"What about crossbows?"

"A risk you need to take, the people's love is more important."

Solineus laughed, half-hearted at first, but the action pulled at the locks sealing his emotions until giving way, and he raised his arms, clapping, pumping his fists. Celebrating felt good, maybe he should try it more often. The power of joy. He whooped and hollered at a group of youths chanting Hîmr's name. "Hîmr!"

Morik shook his head, but after another twenty strides joined him in his shouts and excitement. Men pounded their chests, women threw him flowers, and children rode on the shoulders of their parents just to catch a glimpse of a passing hero: Him. Solineus, Hîmr's Breath. Unreal, yet so real it put air beneath his strides.

The main road was packed all the way through the first gate, but only his party passed this threshold, as guards with halberds and golden helms kept the people from following.

Solineus lowered his arms, exhaled, laughed, and when he spoke his throat threw a worn-out rasp to his voice. "Godsdamn, let's go back and do that again."

Morik chuckled and slapped his back. "That there is a once in a lifetime, my friend, saved for new kings and victorious generals. The people will celebrate for three days."

Solineus pulled a canteen from his belt and drank. "Those pennants… Griffon feathers?"

"Aye. Collected, not taken. The griffon is a holy animal in Helmveline and most of the Kingdoms, unhunted unless they take Kingdomer lives."

Solineus grinned. "So they can eat as many Tek as they like?"

He chortled. "They eat goats, most oft, but stick to the wild herds higher up except in winter, but we keep our herds close during these coldest times."

Solineus hoped he'd see a griffon someday, but from the sound of it, preferred the meeting from afar. "Did I earn a visit to the First Throne today?"

Morik shook his head and guffawed. "Third Throne. Maybe if we hadn't lost half the coin we'd be striding for the third."

They followed the same route to the throne-pyramid and climbed the stairs to find the King and Queen much as they did weeks before, except today they were gowned in pristine white that sparkled as if sprinkled with diamond. A single golden feather hung from each of their necks, its vein long as a forearm. They strode forward, kneeled, and bowed. The stares of the royal couple were similar to the previous meeting.

The Queen spoke: "The Ironwing congratulates your success, but it is sad he must question your failure."

Solineus cleared his throat. "While the Seblêsu made rubs of Hîmr's coin, she…" He'd practiced this a hundred times in his head, but spoken aloud his words felt weak, and he stumbled over them. Desperate, he latched onto one of Morik's sayings. "By the Five Earls, I don't know! She unscrewed part of the blessed thing and left with it, escaping through the Eight Ways of Arumbor's tunnels. It looked as if she rode west, four horses."

"You have these rubs?"

Morik said, "I do."

The queen strode to stand a foot before their faces, and the smell of roses wafted into Solineus' nose. "The coin and rubs, if you will."

He reached into his pocket and retrieved the coin, placing it in right hand, the rubs already in her left. She took the articles to the Ironwing. He examined the coin before placing it in his lap, then twisted a wire and opened a scroll. He stared for two wicks before saying a word. "What should we make of a priestess stealing a piece of such an artifact?" The king's eyes raised, boring into Morik.

"After sharing words with the locals, we know she was from the Kingdom of Barkush."

The king flexed his fingers, agitated. "To what end? All know it was a man in service to Helmveline who claimed the coin, this theft would dishonor the crown. I thought to say she sought to hide something on the back of the coin, but these rubs prove otherwise."

Solineus said, "If I may… could there have been some message inside the coin?"

The Ironwing grinned. "Indeed. But what kind of message?"

Solineus shrugged, then shook his head as well, emphasizing his ignorance. "I know not enough of your lore to guess."

"She risked her life to steal this in front of your open eyes. And the attack?"

Morik's knees shifted and a scowl crossed his face. "Gold masks." Solineus knew this now to mean swords-for-hire. "Not a one who survived could name who hired them, but their goal was Hîmr's Coin."

The Ironwing's fingers balled into a fist. "A distraction? Or a second interested party, do you think?"

Morik said, "My gut says she didn't hire them."

The Queen sat and stretched her legs, head cocked to stare at the coin. "It's worth a fortune even melted into an ingot; some king might wish to possess it even if not rightfully theirs… Does there need be a message?"

Solineus said, "No. But the way she stared at the coin on touching it… hindsight to say I should've suspected something, but, do the other coins twist apart?"

The Ironwing shook his head. "The coins in our possession are this same size and one piece."

"Yet somehow she knew Hîmr's coin came apart. It *must* have a value unto itself, whether it's a message… a map? Directions? Instructions?" He hated the word he was about to utter. "Prophecy?"

Royal brows furrowed, and the king's fist unbound, his fingers drumming the arm of this throne. "I've never heard of a map hidden in such a way, but we can't discount it. No prophecies surrounded the coins… Pîlôstar the Skywind left them as marks of his passing, and as challenges for the holy of the Eight Kingdoms to seek. Nothing more, so far as I know."

Solineus grumbled, this conversation wasn't getting them any nearer to tracking the priestess down. "The symbols on the coin, what do they mean?"

"This is not so easy to say. Hammer, lightning, a single-toothed skull, goat's horn, griffon beak, Rising Sword… they are ancient symbols dating to the God Wars." He leaned, an elbow on the arm of the throne. "What do you know of our history?"

"Only so much as Morik has shared."

"These symbols aren't our written language, they were fashioned in a time after Hîmr and other gods were murdered, and our people fell into ruin and slavery. These symbols have meaning, but to hide the message from dangerous eyes, the meaning shifted with the order of the symbols in a way Forgotten."

"Some scholar must know… have at least an idea?"

The royals shared glances, and the queen answered. "Tulstenar of Hedridôk is wise, if he still lives."

Morik's voice came soft. "He was hunched and ancient last he passed our way, and that two decades past."

The Ironwing said, "We've had no word of his passing. You should seek him out." The Ironwing handed the coin and a single rolled rub to the Queen, and she brought them to Solineus.

He took them with a bow and placed them deep in his cloak. "I will, again, need a guide."

The Queen placed her hand on Morik's head. "It seems you two are bound together."

Morik didn't protest, but his tightened.

Solineus sympathized but would never let the man know it. "And if we find some clue, what then?"

"You send a pigeon to me, track the priestess down, kill her if need be, and return the lost half of coin. If she survives, by all means, send her along as well." The Ironwing stood, opened an ornate chest beside the throne and withdrew two cloaks sewn with golden griffon feathers, and walked to Solineus. "Stand you men, who have done such service for Helmveline, and who seek to do so much more."

Solineus glanced to Morik; the Kingdomer was wider eyed than when he'd found the bolt sticking from his shield. The man held out his hands, so Solineus did the same, and the Ironwing draped the cloak across his arms before giving the second one to Morik.

Solineus didn't know how honored he should be, but Morik's frozen stare suggested he should say something. "I am honored that Ironwing entrusts us with such an honor."

"*Mîhemnar Il-lestir,* words in the old tongue which mean 'men of the holy griffon'. Their weight on your shoulders will see you through cold, rain, and snow, and legend says help you take wing in a strong wind… but they will open

Tulstenar's door as well as the coin, without needing to show the coin until in his presence."

Solineus bowed, and the Ironwing placed a hand on his shoulder. "Drink and feast tonight, as our pigeons seek word on her travels. We will take a day to find her route, then you will seek Tanzarêu the Huntress, so she may lead your way to Hedridôk upon Kingdomer Roads, under the auspices of the Holy Griffon Ilîzô herself."

{❋❋❋}

In a previous life, Solineus would've considered a pigeon an emergency meal when he couldn't get his hands on a chicken. Helmveline esteemed pigeons as a crucial means of communication, going so far as to nickname them the cousins of Griffons. Birds weren't eaten (by Kingdomers at least) and if they managed to evade hawks and other hazards for a decade of service, the birds were retired to live out their natural lives in cozy coops. And the folks who raised and trained pigeons lived well, earning coins from everyone who desired a message sent.

It was one hells of an enterprise.

Kingdomer pigeons were fascinating. Beautiful birds, blue-gray and sometimes mottled white, with purple tints reflecting the sun. Watching them fluff and puff and preen brought to mind the Luxuns, but the pretty and nostalgic paled before their utility of bearing messages from point to point.

As he understood it, Kingdomers toted a crate of pigeons to the Choerkin tent, the Warlord's tent… that would take some getting used to… and all they had to do was strap a note to the pigeon's leg and let it go. The bird did the rest of the work in coming home to roost.

In Molikîn, Tôltô was the Pigeon-master to the Ironwing, and it was a privilege for Solineus to meet with her. She was a tiny gal in her middle years, judging by a few streaks of gray, and she was nimble on her toes, dancing up and down ladders and stairs which lead to a multitude of pigeon houses. The woman managed a complex system of winged messengers, with birds flying back and forth from thirty-two locations daily, not to mention one-way birds like those the Silone would loose.

The woman handed him a tiny scroll and Morik handed her a piece of silver. He smiled and bowed. "Would it be possible to set up daily pigeons to the Silone?"

"For a fee, and with permission from the Ironwing. And they'd need a Pigeon-master… hired or trained."

"I'm sure that could be arranged. How long would it take?"

"A few months, to start. But mastery takes time." A pigeon fluttered past their heads, circled, and landed on her shoulder to coo. "Excuse me."

"Of course."

The woman walked away, the pigeon hopping to her finger for a treat, and Solineus unrolled the scroll. The message was short, a week old, and printed in tiny letters, but it was all he had.

Fish-lips is writing this for me until my penmanship improves, so I can't really say how much of an awful bore he is. I've been told to tell you my learning comes along well. Alu is to marry next month so practices with her sword every minute she can. The first Helmveliner stone-smiths arrived, and a foundation begun on what folks already name "Choerkin Castle" and this keeps Ivin busy. I will never be a queen, but it looks as if I will get my castle. Fish-face thinks this should make me happy. Lelishen arrived a week back with dignitaries from Yolilcoz, a Woodkin city, but I get kept out of most of the boring stuff. She asked after you and was distressed you traveled the Foundations. Rumors of war to the north are persistent, Teks killing Teks, which pleases everyone.

More the next time they allow me a pigeon.

Your adoring daughter,
Kinesee

Fish-breath wrote that.

Solineus chuckled as he rolled the parchment, then stuck it in his pocket. "Ivin's in for a hellsuva marriage."

Morik said, "Your daughter is a kick to the hungover gut as well? A sweet girl when I met her."

"She's got a fire. But at least they won't wed for over a year yet." He stared east toward the Roemhien pass. Messages by pigeon were one-way for the time being, he'd have to write her a note and send it by horseback. "How long for pigeons to reach more distant Kingdoms?"

Morik tugged his beard. "Ask *her*."

Tôltô stood behind him without his noticing. "If the finest pigeons are available, meaning a royal pigeon house, two days or under, three if the weather is bad."

"I should be able to send you a pigeon then, and have a message sent to the Choerkin or my daughter, and get an answer back in five to six days?"

"As you say. Quicker most often. I would be pleased to pass your news along."

There were other staggering ramifications. "If the Hundred Nations struck Helmveline, every Kingdomer to the furthest stretches of the Foundations would know in two days. Or warning another of an attack."

"As you say. Helmveline got word from merchants of an army marching toward Remden of Ômkinter, and a single pigeon turned a slaughter of Kingdomers into a route of the Nations."

Solineus added pigeon houses to stables full of war horses as the top of his list for Silone survival, but for now it was good to know he wouldn't lose all contact. Then the question struck, and his heart quickened. "Could a pigeon come so far as the Parapet Straits? Near the Edan?"

Her lips curled. "It is better to move messages by stages. Birds over such distances make their own schedules, and are more apt to get killed and eaten, but yes, it could be done."

"I take it the nations don't know of your birds?"

"They are enemies, enemies don't learn our secrets. That you know speaks much of the esteem the Ironwing holds for you."

Her eyes rose to a bird soaring in from the southwest, its leg tied with a yellow string. He sucked a deep breath; yellow meant urgent words. "Bodo, from Hervesh." Tôltô knew every bird's name, far as Solineus could tell.

The pigeon lit with a flutter on a perch with a grain filled feeder, and Tôltô took swift strides to the bird's side. She pulled the string and unfurled the roll; good to realize that pigeon-masters knew many of the secrets passing from Kingdom to Kingdom.

"Your priestess passed through Hervesh this morning along the Urzin Trail. Five with her."

Morik said, "Southwest instead of west as we expected."

Solineus clenched his fist and smiled. "I don't give a damns what direction, it's a direction. Time to ride."

Seven

Kingdom Roads

Sunshine or rain,
warmth or drenching chill,
dusty desolation or vibrant verdant.
Your whims do wander to extremes,
idyllic or pain,
all things a direction,
never the same.
Change is a luxury I cannot share.

—*Tomes of the Touched*

Tanzarêu was a squat woman, maybe in her fifties, with deep brown eyes surrounded by sun-browned wrinkles. A round face sat atop square shoulders, framed by hair so disheveled there was no knowing how long it might be if combed.

Solineus had heard such a mess called a bird's nest before, but with this woman the comparison was appropriate; her clothes were a patchwork of linen strips, greens, browns, and grays, interspersed with sticks and leaves that might've been intentional or stuck there from her last jaunt through a prickly bush.

Folks called her *Izimdwî,* The Huntress, but Morik made sure to note she was much more. She was a Wayfinder. She'd spent her life in the peaks and valleys and caverns of the Foundations, learning the trails and paths of both man and beast for so far as the mountains stretched, but so too did she study Waystones.

Fashioned from a rare mineral, Wayfinders tuned their senses to individual stones and hid them throughout the Foundations, whether high atop peaks or in deep caverns, and no matter where they went, they could find their way to one of these, even through mazes deep in the world.

Solineus called it magic; Morik called it a talent and claimed Kingdomers knew which direction they faced no matter how deep in a cave and how many turns they'd taken. Unless they stumbled on raw Waystone, which when standing close fouled their sense of direction. This all felt peculiar to Solineus, as he needed the sun and stars to guide his direction.

They met the woman four days' ride from Molikîn, outside what could be described as a house of sticks, but it wasn't a house proper. More a lean-to with a haphazard door to keep wind, rain, and snow outside. She greeted them with a sneer, an ugly expression which stuck until they showed her Hîmr's Coin and its missing side.

"And just why *did* the Ironwing entrust two idiots, who allowed the thing stolen, to retrieve it? Eh? You will need more than them fancy swords to bring it back."

"Because I defeated the mountain."

She stared. "I scaled to Hîmr's shrine once but chose not to leave my fool bones amongst the others. It wasn't the mountain which needed beaten. Braving the summit may prove you an idiot instead of your worth."

"You were there?"

"An obsidian pedestal on the Plateau of Stolen Breaths, so I named it. Yes, I was there, it stole the air from my lungs on my first step, but not so far in I couldn't escape. In my wisdom, I uttered my reverence in prayer and departed."

"Maybe this too is why the Ironwing sent me to you. And for your wisdom in finding our way to Seblêsu's destination before she gets there."

"Reasonable. Reasonable. To where does she head?"

Solineus coughed. "We don't know."

She cackled and plopped into a pile of leaves, all but her face damned near disappearing, she was so camouflaged. "So, you say you want me to lead you to some place, but you do not know where. The Foundations are an expanse I've spent decades traveling, I need a destination to lead you anywhere."

Morik said, "We need to get to Hedridôk, quick as able."

"You seek that old bear, Tulstenar?"

"If he understands the symbols on the coin, it might point to where she is going."

She snorted and spat. "Mayhaps it would, mayhaps it would not. What is it you wish him to decipher?"

"Freedom carves."

Her eyes widened. "Oh! I see. Let me see the coin."

Morik handed her rolled vellum instead. She eyeballed the thing as she turned it in her hand. "I always imagined a coin being metal, wood at least, not made from a goat's hide."

Solineus said, "It's a rub, so you can see the symbols on the missing half."

She unfurled the scroll, scrunched her face, raised a brow, then nodded. "Mhhm, yes. Mmmm. Eh? Oh, sure sure." She rolled the scroll, tied it, and tossed it back to Morik. "Worthless. Let me see the coin."

It was Morik's turn to snort. "Worthless? We'll be the judge, what'd it say, woman?"

She held her hand out for the coin. "Come now, the coin."

"What's it say?"

"Gibberish for all I care. The coin." She threw her arms up, let them slap back to her lap. "Fine, it speaks of Hîmr, of course. Nothing else bears a point even if I understood a lick it said. Tell me why she wanted a piece of the coin."

"A map. A message. We don't know." Solineus dug the coin from his cloak but didn't hand it to her. "Do you?" A notion kicked around in his head, brought on by what she called the mountain's peak: Breath Stealer. When her only answer was a shrug, he followed his thoughts aloud. "You erred on naming the summit. The shrine doesn't just steal breath."

Her head bobbed back, eyes in a squint. "Erred? What do you mean?"

"When first I put my head over the plateau, it filled my lungs til I might pop as a tick. Then it stole that breath. Morik told me some people believed Hîmr lives—"

"Cult of the Dark Waters... Yes."

"The air atop the mountain moves in and out, as if the mountain is breathing. *Hîmr* is breathing."

"The god alive." She sucked her breath and leaned forward, fingers twined, elbows on her knees. "You're saying the myth is true?"

"I don't know one Earl from another..." He glanced to Morik, and the Kingdomer nodded. "Seblêsu told us she'd been as far as the Yôgul's Fall, what if she lied? What if she went to the plateau and felt the winds? It doesn't matter what they are, elemental or god, what matters is what she believes. If she believes Hîmr lives... she called me the Survivor of Hîmr's Breath."

Tanzarêu nodded, her expression grave. "If what you say is true our game is wasting time... the coin, please."

Solineus surrendered to the look of worry creasing her face and placed it in her outstretched palms; she brought it to her bosom, breathing deep as her eyes slipped closed. "What the hell's she doing?"

Morik said, "Maybe she has a third eye in the damnedest place."

The woman cackled and her eyes opened wide. "Not so far off as you might think, Mountain Lord! This coin, this disc, is a *Nêerubôlm*, a Tracking Stone in the old tongue, which means the missing piece is a Waystone, a special one.

Waystones must be placed by the one tuned to its energy, but this? Anybody could carry it and a Wayfinder with this stone could track it."

Morik stammered. "Tracking… no one's seen… you're certain?"

"I am. With this piece, we can track the other half no matter where in the world it goes, unless it's destroyed." A cackle peeled from her lips a second time. "She stole a thing impossible to hide, once I'm on the trail."

Solineus smiled, but he hesitated in feeling joy. "She's smart enough to know what she stole, then she knows we can track the Waystone. What's her gamble?"

The Huntress' laughter faded, and she stared at Morik. "She's of the Dark Water, I think we can be certain. How much have you told him?"

"The story of Hîmr, little more."

Her gaze lit on Solineus, firm and unyielding. "The Dark Waters believe Hîmr alive… and now, maybe, I believe so too did Pîlôstar the Skywind who left the coin to be found. No matter what was, it is the what *is* that concerns us. They believe him alive and trapped deep in the world. They devote their lives to finding him."

"But the Waystone is a thing to be found? Not to find anything."

"This is so. Puzzle these pieces for me, Survivor of *Hîmr's Breath.* In the Foundations there are great rivers, rivers of black water pouring south deep beneath the jungles and plains above. They believe one of these rivers leads to Hîmr's prison, they believe if they read the clues right, someday they will find this river. The cult takes its name from its deadly undertaking... Every year, pilgrims take boats to these rivers and disappear in their unknown distances. Nobody knows how many live, nor die, nor even how many take this voyage."

Solineus exhaled. "Nothing good comes of seeking the gods, far as I've seen. But this Waystone..." Gears in his head clicked. "If they find Hîmr they could place the Waystone... With the Tracking Stone, would you know when it's placed?"

"Indeed, I would. The connection would grow stronger."

"So, once it's placed, they'd know where to find it, find Hîmr."

"The Exodus of the Dark Waters would ensue. The members of the cult would journey, and with prayer and pick axes, they'd free the god."

"If the legend is true."

"It is *not* true, Hîmr is dead, but if they believed... Thousands would gather to follow the rivers and die in blackness. Lost to the Kingdoms."

Solineus appreciated the woman's confidence in her own beliefs, but certitude never once dictated reality. His meetings with the Touched convinced him little was impossible. "On the chance Hîmr's alive... From what I've seen, finding and waking a god isn't something I want to be around for." He stood and paced, and her eyes followed his steps.

Morik rubbed his forehead. "We've twenty-two warriors with us, we track this thief and we reclaim the Waystone, and the Ironwing will see to it never being used. Simple. Odds were she never expected us to discover this truth, she can't know we're coming." But his weak smile suggested the shallow depths of his confidence.

Solineus stopped in his tracks. "Can her stone tell where this one is?"

Tanzarêu shook her head. "No."

"Then she can't *know* we know, but she hopes we do."

"What're you jabbering about?"

"Why didn't she wait to steal the whole coin? She didn't need it. If we discovered the secret, she knew we'd use it to track her… we're taking the coin straight to her. If we don't, it sits safe and sound in Molikîn to steal when they need it."

Morik's lips flapped as he exhaled. "Five Earls."

Solineus clapped his hands and smiled. "The solution is simple: We get to her before she's ready for us."

Tanzareu's cackle pierced his ears, and she snorted at the close of her laugh. "This foreigner is smart enough to recognize a trap and dumb enough to still walk into it!"

Solineus smiled. "I've a gift."

Morik tugged his beard and stood straight. "I'm here by order of the Ironwing to return Hîmr's Coin whole. Trap or no trap."

"Mayhap we live, mayhap we die. Together we will find this Waystone and our destinies, and maybe one day the sagas will sing of Tanzarêu and the sticks in her hair."

Eight

Road to Wisdom

The brain, the frame, the lingering refrain
of a past fading and the faded passing.
Was I yesterday the man I am today?
Sometimes, not always,
if so it'd be life sideways, something missed,
with no need to forget. No, and no.
Reaching into the Fire today, because
maybe yes, maybe no, maybe maybe,
it'll matter tomorrow is an old game that young fools,
choosing to never reach old with two hands,
play.

—*Tomes of the Touched*

Solineus' eyes struck open in a stare to find Tanzarêu kicking his heels. The first rays of morning sun shadowed the crow's feet marking her eyes and the craters of her dimples. But it was her smile that raised the question. "What'd you find?"

"I think I know where she's a headed."

Morik and several warriors sat up and took note. She knelt and spread one of her maps on the ground, pinning the corners with a couple rocks.

"I'm listening."

"We know she started at the Twelfth Foundation here." Her finger drug west. "Easy to guess she headed west, southwest, but sensing her path… Her path turns often, and it's difficult to tell where she's at, she made a hook that damned near turned her a full circle before moving on west. Judging by that shape, her time of travel, I think she's on the Jakôbin Road." And her finger landed next to a symbol Solineus couldn't read.

Morik said, "You think she's heading for the Wisdom Cliffs?"

"I do."

"Why?"

"I look like the All-Knowing?"

Solineus snorted at the two. "Seems to me she'd be seeking wisdom, given the name."

Tanzarêu cackled and wiped her mouth of spittle. "Your foreigner pain in the ass has a straight way to a point."

Morik grinned. "But what wisdom? The cliffs are histories, but not so far back."

"Mayhaps, mayhaps. I've been through the region a score of times, it's a prime pass through the Foundations, between Mount Gerfôld and Mount Hermin. There are many directions from which to leave its path."

Solineus stood. "All this is blather. How fast can we get

there?"

"Her way is winding and in places steep, assuming she keeps to the wagon roads. We can make better speed, but… best route I know would bring us to the top of the cliffs, and we aren't eagles to swoop down and take her. And if she turns? Then we could lose days."

"No way down those cliffs?"

"Not by hoof. The horses would need backtrack four days to reach the Jakôbin Road."

"Our best horse-friendly route?"

She spat, stared at the map and its myriad of squiggles and marks. "Puts us maybe three days behind them by the time we reach the Wisdom Cliffs."

Solineus glanced to Morik and back to Tanzarêu. "You're saying we risk losing a single day to maybe catch her? Sounds worth it."

Morik grunted. "A day isn't a short time in these mountains. Taken us two weeks to get as close as we are."

Solineus said, "Two weeks, and worst case we're within four to five days behind."

Tanzarêu cackled. "Worst case, we die and never make it. But I think the gamble is good."

Morik groaned to his feet, lifted his saddle to his shoulder. "That be the case, we're wasting sun."

They broke camp in under a half candle and pushed their horses hard as they could into the mountains, swinging south from the road they'd been following to navigate a climbing ridge that twisted and wound until they headed more or less east by evening. Bushes grabbed at the legs of the horses, and branches swatted at Solineus' face in a routine of attacks, so that by the end of the day his muscles were sore from leaning to and fro in the saddle.

The next day was the same, and he blocked more and dodged less, until he surrendered and eased his helm onto his head, letting its cheek and nasal guards keep most of the branches from his skin. Five more days in the saddle trailed into one another, the scenery changing but the same, with snow-capped mountains visible through gaps in the trees surrounding them. Up and down and up again, the monotony broken by scaring up flights of birds, snakes with rattles on their tails, or noting a mountain lion staring at them as they passed. Beautiful animals with huge eyes, so serene while sitting above mouths full of teeth.

But no one fretted the big cats, too smart to attack a train of armored horsemen, and they killed the snakes dumb enough not to slither away and claimed their tails as children's toys; what the Kingdomers watched for was scat left by Ôgrihîn, giant mannish beasts who threw rocks and trees if you passed too close to their cave-homes. Morik claimed the things could take a horse in its arms and squeeze the life from it. Which meant they were bigger than Colok. Which meant Solineus didn't care to meet one.

They reached the top of the Wisdom Cliffs the seventh evening after beginning the journey. Tanzarêu dismounted and Solineus followed, ginger steps to an edge that fell straight to a rock and bramble floor untold strides below.

A great valley stretched from the base of the fall, the land across the road thick with brambles and evergreens. He kicked a rock and watched it plummet over the edge until it clattered on rocks below ten flickers later.

"You weren't joking about the height." The mountain itself wasn't as high as the Twelfth Foundation, but these cliffs were a match for anything he'd seen on those heights.

"There're worse in the Foundations, but once so high… dead is dead at the bottom."

"A practical outlook. Did we beat the priestess here?"

She held her palm out, and he handed her the coin. She pressed it to her chest, then turned a circle with the disc held out. "The Waystone is close, but are we certain she carries it? The other question is will we beat its arrival to the bottom?"

Four Helmveliners took the string of horses back the way they'd come to catch a trail that'd take a friendlier route to the bottom. When Tanzarêu stopped to point out the rubble-scattered goat trail she intended them to descend, he wondered if he shouldn't have stayed with the horses. "That's ummm—"

"Not so bad as it looks, I promise. Take her slow and hug her tight. We'll rope us together, not we need to, and we'll all make it alive. Might leave some skin behind, but alive. I've climbed this a dozen times, plenty of cracks for holds."

Every man cinched rope around their waist and within wicks they started their descent. What started as terror turned to gut-clenched monotony, easing step by step down the path. Centuries before, when fresh-carved into this face, he assumed the trail would've been safer, why else make it? But then, he realized they scaled past runes carved into the mountain, the language of the Kingdomers. He glanced to Morik; a bad idea, the man was below him, so a flicker later his eyes pinned back to the rock face.

"These are the Wisdom Cliffs then?"

"Aye. Some date to the Age of God Wars. It is how we know of some of the battles."

"We're climbing down history, then."

Morik chuckled. "Indeed. It is because of these cliffs that we know there were three Forgettings."

"The Edan believe there were at least five."

"Five Earls, Five Forgettings... Sure, why not? But during the age that Pozorak the Carver marked the victory of King Estwân over a Hundred Nations army on walls just south of here, dating it as the one hundred and twenty-ninth year of remembered time. Then another Forgetting struck, and the carving was found again! And they knew that what they experienced happened before, and every year after they've carved a calendar of years between Forgettings with messages and histories so not everything is forgotten again."

"A wise people." Solineus stopped to scratch his nose, leaning to hug the wall tight. "So, who are these Five Earls? I gather they were hard to tell apart?"

Morik and others laughed. "They are of a tale from these ages."

"Please, distract me from the heights."

"You're serious? Here, now? Seems a thing to wait for reaching the bottom."

"If I fall, I'd hate to die not knowing."

Tanzarêu yelled up at them, "If you fall, you'll dangle; no one dies today, not from a fall no how."

Men laughed and Morik drew a deep breath before beginning. "The Earls are a legend from the Age Between Ages, after Bodomyûl's Wrath and the beginning of our counted time. In the Kingdom of Kâmar the Mountain Lords were then titled Earls, and they were second only to the King in power. On a distant mountain a young warrior called Devêr was rising, nobody knew from where he came, but this wasn't so unusual in these times. What was unusual was how he defeated his enemies with genius plans, outwitting warlords and kings at every turn, until Lobrôd the Fourth, King of Kâmar proclaimed him the Earl of the Seventh Foundation.

"But Devêr was an ambitious Earl. He took the king's daughter for his bride, and on their wedding night, while drunk, King Lobrôd asked how it was he defeated his enemies, as if he knew their tactics beforehand. And Devêr, stumbling drunk, told the king, 'It is because I can be in five places at once, spread across the battlefield, even behind my enemy or in the enemy's camp. Watching, listening, their every step is mine.'

"The King laughed and declared him a drunken fool, but Devêr was not to be mocked. And he said, 'I will prove here and now that you are the fool, not I.' The king seethed at such an insult, but Devêr pushed further. 'There are five of me and only one of you, if true your crown is mine, if a lie you may have my head.' Mind you, the king was bury-your-head drunk, and angry atop that. He lifted his axe from his throne and stomped to stand in front of the Earl. He hefted the axe and said, 'Agreed! You've ten grains of sand before I split your skull.' Devêr pointed behind the king, and when Lobrôd looked… The Earl sat on his throne, and this Earl pointed to a balcony, where stood a third Earl, and this one, to another. Four Earls, and the King said, 'That is not Five.' He bellowed and swung, but a grip from behind latched his wrist, and the axe hit the floor. Earl number five smiled, and plucked the crown from the king's brow, placed it on the First Earl's head.

"Lobrôd the Fourth was no longer king, and King Devêr, first of his name, banished the old man from his kingdom."

Solineus chuckled as he scooted further down the trail. "Hells of a tale for children."

"It is a fine fable for children, but many claim it true. It is carved in the Cliffs of Wisdom. The Earl ruled as king for five decades. Ten years in, they buried an Earl, but there was another. When they buried the second, there was a third, then a fourth, until they buried the Fifth Earl and there were no more."

"You're shittin' me, you believe this?"

"They say no one ever saw the Five Earls together again, but he'd appear in towns and mines around the Kingdom while he was known to be elsewhere." Morik grinned. "Most say Devêr was five brothers who looked the same, of course, but others claim magic."

Solineus laughed. "I met a Tek Duke once…" But his mind spun to a man who would be King: Lord Priest Ulrikt. A man tucked in a casket and thought dead only to return. Could he have had a double? He scoffed at himself. *Don't matter none.* Those worries were long past. He hoped.

Either way, the story distracted from the harrowing shimmy down the cliffs, but the tale should've been longer with such a distance to climb. The sun headed toward the western peaks by the time they set foot to the road, and his stomach growled with a ferocity, but Tanzarêu declared there was no time to eat before their quarry arrived.

Kingdomers crossed the road to scatter among trees, bushes, ravines, and rocks, and he followed Tanzarêu and Morik into a well-shaded cut in the stone hollowed by centuries of water. "How long?"

Tanzarêu held the coin, eyes closed. "Difficult to tell. I've learned much, but how precise my senses I do not yet know."

Solineus cast his eyes the way they came, struck first by how they'd made it down such a treacherous climb, but was forced to reconsider. The path they'd taken was crazy, perhaps, but less crazy than others. Kingdomer runes carved into the cliff's face were tall as a man, and in areas there were paths zigging and zagging which had no track to the top nor the bottom of the cliffs. Far as he could tell, the route they'd taken was the only one which spanned top to bottom.

"Folks who carved those histories… they dangled over the cliffs by rope?"

Morik nodded. "By chain, so it wouldn't fray. Lore speaks to them lowering platforms to base their work from. The workers sometimes slept on these platforms, living there weeks at a time. Dozens of them scurrying like spiders to hurry their job done while foremen below directed their chisels."

"Astounding what men may do when pressed to it."

"Pressed! They were honored to work these cliffs."

Solineus caught the glares of several men and raised his hands. "Not what I meant… I mean, I'm always impressed by what men may achieve when working together."

"This is so." Morik nodded, and all eyes seemed to forgive Solineus' slight.

Figuring it best to keep his mouth shut, Solineus reached into his bag for a hunk of jerky. Besides, no reason for his grumbling gut to give their position away. He chewed, waited, chewed some more, and wondered if maybe the woman's senses weren't as awry as her hair. Clopping hooves echoed off the cliff wall, arriving long before a vision of the oncoming riders. The sound grew and grew, and he realized it wasn't simply because they came closer; far more than six sets of hooves, dozens more.

The voices of two men carried over the racket, and as they rounded the bend, there were six horses riding across, the riders in black robes with their faces hooded and dipped against the bright of the afternoon sun. Six more, and six more, and six more… they just kept coming, all robed in black.

He pressed his body to the rocks, praying gravity pulled him so tight that none of these bastards would see him. Casual words passed between the hooded people, as if they were out for a morning ride before brunch, eighteen rows of six in all, and not a one showed their face. The only thing to wholly prove they weren't some mirroring mirage was that some sat bigger or taller in the saddle, that and the variety of weapons over their shoulders, hanging from their hips, or dangling at the saddle. He assumed they were a holy sect, the question was, were they Dark Waters? From what he'd gathered, he didn't think they'd ride in the open as such, at least not in Helmveline mountains.

One hundred and eight riders, and no way for him to know if Seblêsu was anywhere in the field of black wool. The question mattered, but how to ask it? He glanced to Tanzarêu, scrunched his face and raised a hand, and got a nod… but he didn't know if she answered the question he wanted to ask, so he slumped back into the rocks and eyeballed the tail of the group until they passed over a rise and disappeared. So much for an ambush and quick return to Molikîn.

"Shits."

Tanzarêu stared at him. "There are plenty of rocks and bushes if you need to squat."

Solineus stared back; it took a flicker. "No, it's something we Silone say when were angry. A curse of sorts."

"Oh!" She nodded. "In that case, shits for sure. You boys told me she rode with five."

"That's what the pigeon said. Was Seblêsu in this group?"

The Huntress shrugged. "No way to know, but the Waystone rode between the fourth and tenth row, I think." The other Helmveliners crowded around them, to a man eager to hear their words.

Morik said, "Even with surprise we're no match for that. The Viper's Tongue would be pressed to offer a strategy. And our horses are days away. So, what the hells do we do?"

Tanzarêu cast her eyes in the direction of the Waystone. "We follow; by we, I mean I follow them, and you follow me. When they spot me, it'll be nothing unusual. A Wayfinder in the wilderness by her lonesome. You boys stay well behind me. Eh?"

She took a step, but Solineus grabbed her shoulder. "The coin."

The woman reached into her mess of camouflaged cloak and handed him the tracking-stone, then clucked her tongue twice with a smile and set off at a trot. As she disappeared over the rise, Solineus said, "What if she's one of them?"

Morik squinted. "I guess you just got us all killed by demanding Hîmr's Coin, that the case." He tugged his beard and shifted his weight. "You don't think?"

Solineus tapped the buckle holding the Twins to his shoulders and put his hands to their hilts after they dropped to his waist. Soft, wordless murmurs. If the Twins knew anything, they weren't saying. "I don't think so. Come on, she told us to follow."

When they topped the rise the Huntress was nowhere to be seen, and his heart pounded until he caught a glimpse of movement. He hadn't stopped to consider the challenge of following someone who disappeared into the trees like a bark-spotted sparrow.

They followed Jakôbin Road's rises, falls, and turns for a couple horizons, the cliffs on their left-hand half covered in Kingdomer histories he couldn't read. But no matter, as most times his eyes were peeled ahead trying to stick to Tanzareu's back. As they neared a turn, he spotted her all right, running back to them.

His hands flew to the Twins and his eyes sought cover or high ground for a fight, but as archers scrambled and others planted their feet, no one came for her in pursuit. She stopped, held her hands up, lowered them, then turned and disappeared back around the corner.

Solineus straightened his back, fingers relaxing on the Ikoruv grips of the Twins, as he glanced to Morik. "What the hells was that?"

The Kingdomer squinted into an orange sunset, the final bright of the day cutting down the valley between two snow-covered peaks. "I think they've stopped." He turned to his men. "Take positions here, in case, crossbows bolted and swords light in their sheath. This man and I will see what the Huntress found."

They pressed tight to the corner of the cliffs and peeped

around its bend but saw nothing more than another turn. Morik glanced up at the histories carved above their heads. "I might know where we are."

But he didn't elaborate, leading them to the next bend in the road. From here the hundred and eight were clear to see, but more to his curiosity, a woman stood in her saddle with hood thrown back, red hair blowing in the mountain breeze as she stared at the words high above.

"Seblêsu."

Morik nodded. "They didn't take this route to get somewhere else, she's reading the *Lie of the Raging Eye*, if I know my place in these cliffs."

"What's that?"

"A famous story during the Age Between Ages. A warlord convinced his people that he spoke for the Storm Eye, and convinced them that the tranquility, the calm of the eye of the storm, instead rages. This warlord led four Kingdoms on a crusade against the Tek to reclaim a holy monument, the Stone of Emf'hul."

"A war for a rock?"

"No one remembers what the Stone of Emf'hul is or was or if it's a real thing, but because of this cliff we know Warlord Remshour led tens of thousands to their doom near the Orstân Rift. They say their bones may still be found there."

"What the hells would this have to do with the Dark Waters?"

"I don't..." He pointed, and Solineus' eyes took flickers to pin what he pointed at.

"What the hells is Tanzarêu doing?"

The woman skulked through brush and trees north of the group, closer than Solineus felt comfortable. She dropped and lay flat. Gone. And a flicker later he realized why. A man in black robes strode between rocks and around bushes, hiked his robes and pissed. If he spotted the woman, they all might be dead in a flare.

"How doesn't he see her?" The stream couldn't be more than a foot from her toes.

"I've stepped on hunters wearing their gear before seeing them. That'll give you a start, I promise."

The robed man finished and turned back to the party, and flickers later a piece of brush raised its head. "She's good."

"Indeed. And I wager, she's on our side."

Tanzarêu stood and slunk back to the road, but instead of coming their way, she turned toward Seblêsu and the cliff she read. Tanzarêu stood straight and tall as she walked, no longer hiding.

"You sure of that?"

"I'm sure. As she said, no reason they'd suspect her of anything."

The Huntress hailed the group, raising her arms in greeting, and they welcomed her. Solineus' heart raced. "Guess we'll know in a wick or two."

A conversation ensued between Tanzarêu and a broad-shouldered man, the only one to dismount and lower his hood on the Huntress' arrival. She pointed Northeast, and he heard her cackle, then she pointed southwest and straight west. They clasped forearms, and the man bowed when they let go.

A flicker later Tanzarêu wandered from the road, into the brambles and stones, disappearing.

"We're still alive."

They crouched, waited, and watched. Seblêsu pointed at the cliffs, and he almost made out her words on the wind, but they were a tease. Then her hand circled above her head and any who'd dismounted put foot to stirrup and lifted into their saddles. Hoods pulled over the few uncovered heads, and in a flicker the train moved out, slipping into neat rows of six as they rode.

Morik led him back to the rest of the Helmveliners and they gathered in a loose group of nervous eyes and shuffling feet awaiting Tanzareu's return. The Huntress appeared on the road, a crooked tree making her way from a backdrop of crooked trees until she stood in front of them, a grin on her face.

Morik asked, "What next?"

The woman grunted. "We wait for our horses, then we follow them to Shînvedorn."

"They told you where they're headed?"

"No. They didn't need to."

Solineus fought back an impatient snarl. "What the Earls are you saying?"

"They asked the quickest route to Elimmor, but the *Lie of the Raging Eye* is what they stopped to read."

Morik stomped a foot. "The Raging Eye doesn't speak of either place."

"Indeed, no, but it does say: 'Warlord Remshour knelt before the Sundial of Teremhôst in prayer, and at high-sun did the shadow point to the Stone of Emf'hul, marking the time and place for holy war.' So the story tells."

"And they marched to the Orstân Rift to die. What's your point, woman?"

Solineus rubbed his forehead with a chuckle. "And recall I'm foreign to all of this."

"Not so foreign as you might think if I'm right." Tanzarêu grinned. "And besides, we've got time to study and learn… days before the horses arrive. Morik, Mountain Lord, for what was Remshour's Crusade fought?"

"The Stone of Emf-hul."

"This is what our historians teach. For *what* was it fought?"

"You're making me feel a fool, woman. Speak plain."

"I'm thinking this through with you—"

"The gods." Solineus' lips flapped before he'd thought it through, but everything he'd experienced since awaking on a beach pointed to this one thing. "And power."

"This foreigner knows, but knows not enough. Some things are always left unsaid for the wise to puzzle, are we wise? What would be worth four Kingdoms going to war in a foreign land? The power of the gods… a god, trapped in the mortal world."

Morik's head cocked. "You're saying Remshour founded the Dark Waters in the Age Between Ages?"

"Mayhap, mayhap! And what do they need to find Hîmr, the Stone of Emf-hul."

She pointed at Solineus and he said, "A tracking-stone."

"And its Waystone mate. Our barbarian friend recovered the Stone of Emf-hul, little did he or most anyone else know."

Morik glanced back and forth between them. "Five Earls, it makes sense. Except the war they fought was in the Great Canyon, the Orstân Rift."

"Pîlôstar the Skywind found the stone in *our* Remembered Time and put it atop Hîmr's Shrine."

Solineus snorted. "Back to the now… Assuming all this true, what the hells this got to do with them being headed to Shînvedorn?"

Tanzarêu cackled. "First, they asked for directions to Elimmor, as opposite in direction to Shînvedorn as you might get. Two, the Sundial of Teremhôst is near Shînvedorn."

"Why the Sundial?"

"It pointed a direction once." She shrugged. "And it was mentioned several times as I watched."

Morik said, "They wouldn't need to stop here just to reference some Sundial."

She breathed deep, exhaled with an exasperated smile. "Indeed. And we have three days of staring at the cliffs to figure it out."

In the forty-fourth year of this Age, Warlord Remshour defeated the Kemindûl at the battle of Trênswân, and so claimed the Black Fingered Pool known as the Sundial of Teremhôst. Here he claimed his own greatness, beneath the lightning skies of thunderheads, and claimed the greatness and anger of the Storm's Eye, that there was no longer an eye, but all storm. The priests of Mônvêur came and pronounced his words. The priests of Gîhon came and pronounced his words. On the twelfth day of the twelfth month the high sun came and the Black Finger pointed its shadow crooked into the lands of the barbarian kings.

And the priests prayed, and the Oracle of Menzên declared the Stone of Emf-hul found in the Temple of the Great Rift, and her visions would lead their way. Four armies came, and four armies remained, four kings unconvinced.

Remshour rode at the head of his army with holy lightning and lava-forged hammer in hand, and smote the barbarian horde of Mitêz. He smote the barbarian king Remîsh by his own hand and threw down their fortress city. He smote the gates of the city of Kîimor with lava-forged hammer and his army put every barbarian to the blade. He reached the Great Rift and met the armies of Hulumbor, and was smitten by the beauty of this king's daughter, and her knife through his chin to exit his eye.

And Remshour's armies were slaughtered, fled, or captured and enslaved. Remshour lived, one-eyed and chained above the gates of Hulumîsis, on his knees and pecked by birds until he died a prisoner and slave to the woman who became Queen of Hulumîsis. Decades of humiliation and agony later, he died. His flesh rotted. His bones remained. A warning above the gates to any who might try the power of the Hulumbor.

Nine

Crooked Finger Black

The city will rise so long as the walls never fall,
the tide a forever rise to swell beneath moon full,
a life immortal waiting for the sweet nail to impale,
Cry why fly sky deny sigh vie why Cry?
Nigh, Naive.
Tears fall because there's only one direction to go.

—*Tomes of the Touched*

They stared at the cliffs for three and a half days before the horses arrived, and when they swung into the saddle and heeled toward Shînvedorn they were as ignorant of why Seblêsu stopped at the cliffs as they were the flicker they read him the history.

Solineus stretched his legs, rising in the stirrups. "Maybe they knew they were being followed and stopped here just to twist our heads around."

The Kingdomers laughed but to a one they knew there was something there. Something in those words hidden. But finding it left them grasping for codes or cryptic imagery, Black Finger and Crooked Shadow.

They pushed the horse hard that first day as they were well-rested, but eased off as their journey wound into a high pass between Mount Gerfôld and Mount Hermin, two lop-sided peaks which seemed to lean away from each other, as two friends parting, or two foes turning their backs to the other.

The air grew chill the day they crossed these heights and the wind howled, but they descended into a green valley after. They made camp around village wells and in the mouths of mines as they could, but they no longer traveled mountains held by the Helmveline. They sheltered with the people of Kingdom Tûrûrôt and spoke not a whisper of their mission, nor asked after the party of black robes they tracked.

Still they caught word; a band of holy folks a hundred strong brought a waggle to tongues in the same way their passing would be spoken of once they were gone. The words of both Tanzarêu and the townsfolk put Seblêsu's lead at two days by the time they reached the village of Ekwumor. It'd been three weeks of winding travel to gain two days, which meant Seblêsu and her people might be riding through the gates of Shînvedorn even as they spread their bedrolls for the night.

Tanzarêu held the coin facing west that evening, and again in the morning. There was no surprise in her tone. "The Waystone hasn't moved since yesterday afternoon."

The next night they camped inside the dark maw of a natural cavern high enough to bring a deep chill to his bones. When gaps formed in the clouds Morik pointed to a walled city sitting in a distant valley, a score of round towers rising from low walls: Shînvedorn.

Tanzarêu spoke with a smile this time. "The Waystone hasn't moved."

They celebrated their arrival in Shînvedorn with a hot dinner at an inn with a giant tavern in its belly. Their meal was four courses of meats, each spicier than the last, and topped by heavy, dark ale. Morik paid for all their rooms before the three of them stepped from the tavern and into the street.

Solineus gawked; he couldn't help himself. Tanzarêu wore a dress, simple but clean, and had somehow managed a comb through the knots on her head. She wouldn't pass for a noble, but for a time she didn't pass for a tree.

She caught his lingering gaze. "What do you think you're staring at?"

"Funniest looking tree I ever did see."

Her cackle was the same as ever. "Come, let's see what we can find." She patted the pouch holding the coin around her neck. Or rather, the Stone of Emf-hul, if the lady were right.

Solineus rested his hands on the hilts of the Twins to the murmur of whispers; along with burying their griffon-cloaks in the bottom of their packs, Morik had made him wrap the hilts of the Twins in leather to make their value less obvious, less gossip worthy, but the Twins didn't seem to mind if ever they noticed.

Shînvedorn wasn't a gargantuan city, but neither was it short of people and winding streets. The wealth arose from being the hub of a mining wheel, with spokes coming from a dozen or more mines in the region. Gold, silver, precious gems, and some infused-ores like Ikoruv, though veins of these precious commodities were scattered and scarce. Tanzarêu led them down Smelter's Way then crossed onto Hammer Street, where bellows pumped and hammers rang.

Morik bore a shit-eating grin. "You could find yourself a fine shield here."

Solineus grinned back. "You paying for it?"

"Pain in the coin purse friend, thinking that's worse than a pain in the ass."

"You boys hush, I'm trying to focus."

Solineus gave her a stare. "You can shake the dust from the bush, but you can't take its thorns."

"I'll show you thorns in a flicker, barbarian. Now hush." But the woman smiled as she sauntered to a pole hung with horseshoes and other iron goods. Her hands on the pouch meant she wasn't shopping. She nodded south and led them onward.

"How far is it? A guess?"

"Can't say. Cities like this are spotted with Waystones, it complicates things. In the wilderness it's a beacon, here it's merely the brightest star in a crowded sky."

But it hadn't moved in days, leastwise not enough the Huntress noticed. She wandered from Hammer Street into Armorers Row, then took a turn down an alley while holding the pouch. When next they came to a street, it was broad, crowded, and running across the front of the gates leading to the cities great keep.

"What is it you barbarian squatters say? Shits?"

Morik sighed. "She's in the Keep of Shînvedorn?"

"The stone is, and I doubt she's far away. Which all means she's friends we'd prefer not anger."

Solineus leaned against an empty wagon and stared. The gate was wide open but guarded by four men with halberds. "We go in, or wait for the coin to come out?"

The woman cackled. "Your barbarian is bold. We wait. These bones got no desire to find themselves flayed for breaking into some lord's tower."

Solineus snorted. "Time to rest won't hurt none of us… This city have pigeons?"

Morik said, "Indeed. We should get word back to the Ironwing… and your daughter."

Tanzarêu let the pouch fall against her breast as she turned and led them east. "I know the pigeon-master her, a fine old gal, we can send your messages before settling in for the night."

❦❦❦

The next morning Solineus found Tanzarêu in the tavern at the break of dawn, and as he sat, she whispered with a wink and nod. "The stone hasn't moved."

He smiled at this excellent news. For a week straight he smiled at these words every morning and night. After ten days, his smile waned, and after a month she didn't bother to update him every day. Worse, Morik grew cranky as his pouch emptied feeding and housing so many men.

On the bright side they'd spent enough time in one place to receive word from Kinesee:

To my Father,

Alu married! And she has yet to slay her groom, that's the biggest news so far as I am concerned. I think I almost died when teasing her about having babies. A subject I don't recommend the unarmed broaching for some time.

The foundation to the new wall and its towers are in the ground. Helmveline workers arrived not long after my last letter, claiming they owed you a debt, and went to work with an uncanny speed with stone-saws and chisels, logs for rolling and clever contraptions for raising blocks high. I never understood the sweat nor know how needed to build such things, and I spend much time watching them work.

Of late I spend hours with the pigeon-master who arrived from Molikîn and already she has eggs resting in a nest in the cliffs by where Castle Choerkin will stand. She is young and tolerates me as I hide from my learning.

Today I write in my own hand, but the odious Ravinrin boy persists in correcting my spelling. If I have erred in any words, please punch him in the nose on your return.

Kinesee

Most of the pigeons sent were for more serious matters, including the Ironwing sending Morik a voucher for gold. Solineus wasn't certain how such a thing worked, but the Kingdomer was able to exchange the note for three bricks of bullion, which the local repository changed out for coins struck by a Tûrûrôt mint. With this, food and shelter were no longer a worry, growing complacent and fat were.

Solineus strolled the streets of Shînvedorn every day, passing the gates to the keeps several times morning, noon, and sundown hoping to get lucky, to see Seblêsu leaving the gates. He determined that he'd used up his luck by staying alive.

Sixty-three days after arriving, Solineus sat in front of a crackling fire, legs stretched, chin tucked, and damned close to a happy snore when Tanzarêu shook his chair so hard he clutched its sides to keep from sprawling to the floor.

She spoke under her breath, but her tone was fury. "The stone. It's gone."

"What the shits are you talking about? Where to?"

"Gone, not moved. If they've taken it, I have no idea where to."

Solineus' heart raced, but what she said wasn't true. "The Sundial."

Within a candle the twenty-five rode from Shînvedorn to follow a winding easterly trail, until it hooked south the second day. On the third morning they reached the edge of the Foundations, or at least he witnessed his first view not encompassed by mountains since following Morik to Shuntiskâ.

The mountains fell steep into a thick woodland, and from these heights he could make out sweeping plains further to the south. From his vantage, the lands seemed so flat it didn't belong to his world, with its river sweeping back and forth across the land like some giant snake. All he'd known in his remembered days were mountains and rolling hills.

Tanzarêu turned them west from here and his view returned to peaks as they descended into a deep valley by way of a steep, rocky trail where flat patches were covered with pinecones and fist-sized nuts. She clucked and they all dismounted, walking their horses and clearing the trail.

Solineus kicked a large nut; it hurt his toe, convincing him they might crack a skull when falling from the trees. "If they took this route, it seems odd they didn't clear the way."

Tanzarêu snorted. "Thought the same myself. They aren't here. We were wrong. Which saves us needing sneak."

Solineus' lips pinched. "You best be shittin' me."

"No, we're here. They aren't."

In thirty strides they reached bottom, and a short walk later the trees cleared. A stretch of the mountain's mockingbird-gray slate lay bare to winds and water, a hundred strides long and just as wide in places. A carved divot, a perfect circle with straight edges, stood in the middle of the clearing, and in its center stood what he might've called a stalagmite if he were in a cave. Black and polished to a shine, hints of purple glow suggested it was translucent enough for some light to pass through. It cast a long shadow across the ground, landing on a symbol he didn't understand.

There was nothing crooked about the shadow, and the woman had been correct: No one was here.

He strode to the center of the dial, stepping down two steps and stared as Kingdomers fanned across the clearing. "Obsidian, similar to Hîmr's Shrine atop the mountain. We've got a big black finger and nothing else."

Morik said, "Maybe we've the wrong place?"

Tanzarêu grunted. "Maybe we been thinking wrong all along."

Solineus glanced to the sky. "The cliffs mentioned the high sun; we aren't there yet."

Morik stepped in the shadow the stone cast. "This thing casts a shadow straight as an arrow. What'd make the shadow crooked?"

"A heat mirage?"

"Mayhap, mayhap." Tanzarêu wandered the circle's symbols. "The carves name the phases of the day; dawn, mid-morn… Nothing unusual."

Solineus leaned against the obsidian, wondering if the Touched hadn't a hand in writing the words on the cliffs. *Reckon they weren't cryptic enough.* And he almost laughed aloud, but the humor stuck in his throat. "We're standing in a dry pool. Way this slopes, a rain would fill… The reflection, the rippled shadow, could that be called crooked?"

A flitter of leaves and he froze, uncertain; then Tanzarêu screamed.

Solineus' head whipped to see the woman spin, feathered fletching sprouting from her right shoulder as she collapsed in a heap. The Twins flashed in his hands as he guessed the trajectory; the brother hissed, and he flicked his wrist at the glint of a quarrel heading for his neck. *Slap-tink* and *clatter* the bolt hit the ground. This time Helmveline eyes plied the woods, and the twangs a dozen crossbows sent razor-heads whistling into the trees. A man fled, scrambling up the hill.

He turned to Tanzarêu, profuse blood as her head rested in Morik's hands, and the Kingdomer bellowed in Silone: "Kill that son of a whore!"

He stared at Tanzareu's eyes a flicker; the wound wasn't a kill shot, least not a quick one, but the force of the head if it caught her bone… He spun with a roar, feet sliding as he pushed into a dead sprint, passing the Helmveliners in their heavier gear. He leaped sideways between two trees where he thought he'd seen one man, the Twins high; two bolts stuck from this assassin's chest, his breaths ragged and life fleeting. He cocked an ear, blinking fast as he heard feet scrambling up leaves and rocks. He turned and loped east, eyes scanning every tree and gulley and rock in case there was a third waiting for him. A hundred strides later he spotted the killer; a man in twig covered gear scaled a sheer cliff, snagging vines, branches, and cracks to make his escape.

Solineus sheathed the Twins and grabbed a crevice to climb, but after three steps of height pushed back from the wall, dropping to his knee as he lit and picking up a large nut. He tested its heft with a toss in the air and slung it at the man's head. It hit the man's thigh, making him grunt, and slowing him.

This made him smile.

He picked up two more nuts, clacking them together. "This is going to hurt like a kick to a hungover gut, my friend." He wound up and heaved this time, hard enough to threaten a pain in his own shoulder, but it was nothing compared to what the bastard must've felt. It struck the assassin center of mass between his shoulder blades, eliciting a grunt, and the man dangled by a single hand before regaining a grip.

Three Helmveliner crossbowmen pulled up by his side, cranking their windlasses.

"Seems I got one more chance before they put holes in your hide." He tested the weight and hurled the nut; the hollow crack was one of the most satisfying sounds of Solineus' remembered life as blood spattered on impact with the man's skull. He thudded to the cliff floor about the same time as the nut and rolled to the base of a tree, out cold or dead. "If he lives, bring him back to the clearing."

Solineus jogged back down the hill, zigging through trees and hopping branches until he came to Morik's side as he plied pressure, doing his damnedest to staunch the flow. He kneeled with eyes locked on Tanzarêu. Blood covered the stone, and her body shook.

"Her shoulder's shattered. A healer might save her..."

"Do what you can." But he'd seen wounds enough to know it wouldn't be enough. He glanced back to the trees as Helmveliners strode into the clearing without the assassin. It would've been damned handy to have a living soul to question, but at the same time he was happy the bastard died, and he'd been the one to take his life. He turned his eyes to Tanzarêu, bowed his head and waited for her ragged breaths to slow and fade, to slip into peace. He hadn't known her long, but he liked her more than most.

A good woman.

A good soul.

But a voice in the back of his head voiced reality: She wouldn't be the last he cared for to pass from his life. And he struggled to bury this voice before forced to bury his friend.

❀❀❀

They built a cairn of rocks in the trees, a natural place for the Huntress to spend her eternity, but they left the killers to rot or feed whatever wild animals found them. After, they retired to the clearing, Helmveliners standing guard as Solineus carved Tanzareu's name into a stone as broad as Morik's chest. He felt it the least he could do.

Morik paced. "No way we find them bastards now… we should've had the old man read the Freedom Carves."

Solineus shook his head as the Twin screeched, its tip biting rock. "I reckon she was right, the carves meant shit. We've got a problem to solve, and we need another Wayfinder to solve it."

"We're in Tûrûrôt, and it damned well looks like the whore has friends at the keep. We'd be two-times lucky to find a Wayfinder who wouldn't sell us out. They made sure to kill her, not one of us, for a reason."

Solineus grimaced as the Sister made a painful noise. "Then we godsdamned figure it out ourselves. This site means something."

"It means shit, they set us up."

"Nope! I ain't buyin' it. This place means something. That long dead warlord who sought the stone came here in the first place… why?"

Morik spat and sat. "No one's gonna be able to read her name in Silone, not even me."

Solineus grimaced. "Then you'll just have to show me how to carve it in Kingdomer runes. Why'd the warlord come here?"

"Because the sundial pointed the bastard's way."

"But how'd they know that? We agree all this points to Hîmr's prison—"

"Tomb."

"Hîmr's tomb." Solineus glanced at the black finger of the sundial.

"But there isn't no crooked shadow, lest you want us all to piss and fill the pool, see what happens—"

"Hush a godsdamned flicker." Solineus stopped the Sister in mid-screech. "Hîmr… what gods did Hîmr find to fight by his side as he fled?"

"What the hells that got to do with shit?"

"Your swearing is getting good, my learning you Silone is paying off. But humor me."

Morik chortled. "Godsdamned whoreson… You're right, I'm getting the knack for your tongue! Them gods were Korhânun and Sanzumôk. Both died with him."

"Or maybe imprisoned. All your gods have nicknames… Stabber, stabbed, impaler?"

Morik laughed. "Korhânun the Impaled Pool."

"Thrown down a spear of stone jutting from a pool of water." Solineus pointed the Sister's blade at the sundial, his heart beating fast.

Morik grunted and turned, but whatever he was about to say stayed silent in his drooping mouth. He smacked his lips. "Unholy shits. You're saying—"

"Maybe this is where Korhânun took the wound they say later killed him."

Morik shook his head. "They *say* the battle was underground…"

"Stories say a lot of things. If there was water, what would your eyes see?"

"An impaled pool." He tugged the rings in his beard. "Right, fine and well… Say you're right. What the hells good does it do us?"

"We're following the story of Hîmr to his prison… Sanzumôk? His story?

"*Tomb*. Sanzumôk the Riven Flow. Korhânun was bleeding to death, but fought on, leading them to a river deep in the mountains, a river which split to go around a massive stalagmite pillar. The enemy gods arrived and Hîmr fled down the Dark Waters; the two gods battled their foes,

Korhânun fell into the western current, and Sanzumôk into the eastern. Both dead."

"Or alive to later be imprisoned. The cult is named for them Dark Waters?"

"Aye, it is."

"Somehow, some way, this place is pointing us to the Riven Flow."

Morik jumped to his feet and pointed. "It's a sundial, it points all over the godsdamned place! Do you see a crooked godsdamned shadow?"

"No. No I don't." The Black Finger struck from the mountain's stone with a lean to give a better shadow on the sundial. He stood and wandered to gaze at the obsidian.

Morik followed close. "What the hells you gawkin' at?"

Solineus shook his head, eyes scanning the dial's carvings, nothing unusual, Tanzarêu had said, and he took the woman's word for it. His eyes wandered to the shadow it cast; how to make the shadow crooked? He rubbed his face, stopped with his knuckles pressing his eyes. *We assumed the finger cast the shadow.* He stepped back, then circled to stand straight behind the Black Finger's lean, and his lip curled in a grin. "It points to Mount Hermin."

The mountain angled from its sister mountain, the two leaning from each other, and Mount Gerfôld blocked the sun, turning the other's peculiar shape to shadow. "A shadow pointing southwest."

Morik tugged his beard. "That's a fickle cast of the dice, my friend…"

"Tell me it don't make sense. Get Tanzareu's map."

Within a wick they had the Huntresses map spread on the stone and several Helmveliners circled them. Morik poked a symbol next to an inked mountain: "Mount Hermin. By her drawing, the peak ridge kind of leads this way."

And Solineus unrolled another map, this one of underground caverns and mines she'd explored. "Where's the mountain on here?"

Morik searched, pointed, then drew a line. Stopped with a huff. "Half a dozen underground flows in the vicinity it points."

"Any she shows split in twain?"

"No. And she's got some of these here detailed."

"After all these years, odds on the flow would've cut one side deeper… it might not split no more." He pointed to a river with a scratch to its side. "That her way of marking a ravine?"

"Hells if I know, could've been a mistake she erased… or…" He looked up with a grin. "She named it the Barren Mirror."

"That could mean dried ravine, a split."

"It's better than a shot at the eagle's eye."

"And if we're wrong… we're no worse than afore." Solineus smiled and stood. "The Huntress might have her revenge, yet."

Morik rolled both maps and tied them, spoke to his men: "We ride, and with the Storm Eye's blessing, we will repay the enemy the pain they have wrought nine times fold!"

Kingdomers shouted "Nine times fold!" and banged their shields; Solineus savored the rhythm as it fell in beat with his pumping heart, a heart which now owned a certain and bloody destination.

Ten

Snow Fall

Scoured flower in the dour dowry,
hand in the sand let the fist fly,
world grains blinked to blindness.
Posit: the worlds beyond this world
are closer than the eye can see,
what then the notion that only the White Eyes
are the worlds' witnesses?

—*Tomes of the Touched*

They were three weeks into their journey from the Sundial and on a path set higher in the mountains than Tanzareu's maps had prepared him for. The Kingdom of Tûrûrôt lay behind them by four days; the peoples of these mountains were Ôshô Kingdomers, and to call them reclusive was an understatement. Half the villages closed their gates on seeing foreigners, and Solineus wasn't convinced the other half wouldn't have done the same if they'd seen them coming. Or if they had gates to close.

First, he'd waved to goatherders as he'd done in the past, but to a soul they looked away as if he and the Helmveliners were figments; he learned to ignore them in the same fashion. The Ôshô, Morik assured him, were outliers among the Kingdoms, skittish around everyone. According to tradition, the peoples of this Kingdom were brutalized by slavers during the God Wars, more so than the other Kingdoms, and their priests preached that their Kingdomer kin had some role in this persecution. Five hundred or a thousand years ago or yesterday, it didn't matter: The Ôshô trusted no one. But at the same time, they were fewer in numbers, weaker, and poorer than the other Kingdoms, a condition for which they took no blame, despite limiting trade from outside their borders.

"Speak to any Kingdomer and to a soul they will tell you they hail from the greatest of the Eight Kingdoms! Not so, here in Ôshô. Even their king seems to take a perverse pleasure in their struggles and weakness. Ôshôins both able and courageous, flee these mountains to take home with their neighbors." Morik's opinion of Defin, King of Ôshô, and Thirteenth of his Name, was one of disgust, and it came clear as a whistle that they'd find no help in these mountains.

Solineus stood strides from a cave's mouth as snow sailed over his head in torrents of wind-driven white. It was old snow blowing down from the peak above, but it'd blind them just the same if caught out in the wind's furry. Still, fresh snow would've been worse. He turned and gazed to the back of the cavern where men sat dozing around a fire and horses stood tethered. The tunnel went deeper into the mountain, but Morik assured him there were no signs of Ôgrihîn living here.

He wandered back to the fire. "Reckon Seblêsu is badgered away like we are?" The notion of losing time aggravated him. They'd caught rumor of a band of priests leaving Shînvedorn the same day Tanzarêu died, and it was an easy assumption that the Waystone traveled with them.

"No way to know in the mountains, no way to know which route she even took."

When the winds died the white world disappeared into a brilliant blue sky with a sun bright enough to send his eyes crawling into the back of his head. Morik unrolled a map and took a look before they headed out.

"We move down mountain from here, clipping the border with Barkush. This city here, Faldan, I've heard of. They've trade enough that we'll get supplies before pushing to the caves and the Barren Mirror River."

The route they took was riskier, but faster, than others they assumed a party of a hundred men would take. But what felt like a certainty at the Sundial of Teremhôst felt like extraordinary optimism when holed up in a mountain cave; their choices were fewer than the words he spoke. "We do what we can."

There was a reason he said down mountain instead of downhill: the descent was so steep they were forced to walk their horses in a meandering row down the face of the mountain before reaching a ridge line pulling them due west. And still they walked, the snow deep and the drop on their left hand an unpleasant one.

They trudged through snow for a horizon before it cleared to ankle height, and ahead, he could see a bare-stone trail leading down the mountain. But the scout ahead stood still, scanning the snows. Solineus spoke to Morik: "What's the trouble? Ôgrihîn?"

The scout turned, waving his arms in a series of poses. "Tracks leading up the face yonder. But—"he pointed a field of white above them"—he's more worried about an avalanche."

"What the hells we do about that?"

Morik grunted. "We had time we'd backtrack… But we don't. We press on, silent as we're able. Them godsdamned snows come after us, run like the hells from its path, not down its path. Find a tree or boulder. The snow takes you, swim-like. I've been buried once and survived, so don't panic if it happens."

Solineus grunted as he watched the first Helmveliners make their way one by one across the stretch. "What about them prints?"

Morik shrugged, motioned for silence, and followed the man in front of him by a healthy twenty strides. Solineus stared at his back, then followed with similar spacing. The only noise was hooves on stone. *It's like any other piece of rock, just walk it.* He glanced up the mountain; a patch of black moved. He strode on, uncertain whether to break the silence.

An explosion.

A puff of snow in the heights.

And the world shook.

First everyone froze, then they ran.

Solineus let loose his horse's bridal and slapped the animals flank. "Get!" The gelding reared and bolted, and Solineus followed as lines of snow and ice shivered then broke in shifting waves down the mountain's side.

He heard nothing but the roar of snow tumbling down the mountain as his feet raced over stone, two horses passing him from behind. The avalanche followed a swale which formed a chute down the mountain; best guess, he wasn't going to make it from the path. Close, maybe.

He angled for a boulder, leaped atop; his drumming heart realized this boulder wouldn't save him, and he leaped into the conifer's branches as the snow struck, spraying high then swallowing the giant stone. He clung to branches and scrambled higher. *Crack.* He felt the tree snap as much as he heard it. His tree leaned and he dove into the flow of snow, and as stupid as it sounded, he swam.

But not for long.

The snow buried him, and he brought his hands to his face as he came to a stop, and he did his damnedest to clear space in front of his face. The good news: It wasn't cave black, the snow above was shallow enough to show light.

He took a single deep breath, shoved his right hand high, and thought maybe his gloved fingers reached air.

Relax. The snow only got some of us. They're coming for me. He willed every muscle to melt into calm and breathed shallow, eyes closed.

{❋❋❋}

His eyes remained closed, but he knew the world of ice-white had turned to waves of blues and grays before he opened them. "Is there a reason you come to me when I'm near dead?"

The Lady's sonorous laughter flowed over his skin with tingles, or was that his body dying? "Am I coming to you, or are you coming to me? Not easy to explain… But, the looser your consciousness' tether with your body, the easier we may converse. Near death, a deep dream state…"

"So, if I really need to talk, I should strangle myself?"

"I don't recommend it, my love, but yes. Though it might not work as well as you hope."

He'd hoped the answer to be a blunt no. "Am I dead?"

"How many times will you ask that?"

"Until I'm finally right."

She giggled. "All things that will be have their time, my love."

He sighed. "I'm failing again."

Her beauty faded into existence, the curl of a perfect smile warming his soul. "How can you fail at what you didn't set out to achieve?"

"You wanted me to find allies—"

"The Kingdom of Helmveline calls no foreign people friend *except* the Silone. Because you don't yet understand how much you've achieved, doesn't mean it's any less significant."

He wanted to grab and shake her, or at least to rub his own eyes, but as always, no part of him did more than twitch;

if indeed that sensation was even real. "The Waystone'll be lost—"

"The Waystone is of no consequence to you—"

"Then why the hells are people dying for it?"

"It *is* of consequence to the Eight Kingdoms and the Foundations, but not to you or me."

"The hells you say! These people are my friends and I've *seen* what pursuing the gods has wrought upon a people!"

Her smile and vision faded, and she reappeared beside him, breath warm on his ear. Despite his angered tone, her voice was calm and soothing. "You see, my love? You see now how successful you will be and why? Loyalty begets loyalty. Friendship begets—"

"Friendship." He relaxed as her warmth sifted through his being. "Tell me then, does Hîmr live?"

She sighed, and a chill washed through him, the only warmth her breath. She feared this answer, and so he knew to fear it as well. "Some things are best left undiscovered. Seek things you *should* discover. Go west. Always west until you find your future's past in the city of red domes."

Air moved around his hand, and someone tugged his fingers. "No! Where west, damn it? What city?"

She kissed the ridge of his nose and his eyes fluttered open to bright light and Morik's big teeth staring down at him. "Pain in the ass friend! You live!"

Morik and two others pulled him from the snow's grip, and Morik helped him stumble to the safety of rocks, before going out to find more survivors.

Solineus collapsed against a boulder, every muscle in his body weak, no more capable of holding him steady than pudding. Helpless to help, watching a desperate search. Seven in all were drug from the snow, two dead, and after a candle the search for the remaining four ended. Lost until somé warm summer day.

They tended wounds, chased down horses until they had more mounts than riders, then took shelter in an outcropping of stone surrounded by cedars. The fire crackled as men mourned in their bowls and cups. A few sang to the mountains, and Solineus wished he could join them, but neither his spirit nor body were ready for even a sad song. Hard truths needed spoken.

Solineus looked to Morik. "A stonebreaker brought the snows on us."

The Kingdomer didn't look from his bowl of hot water as he nodded. "She anticipated our route."

"She did." Why did this surprise him so much? "She's been ahead of us since we came down the mountain. Maybe… We should just take the Tracking-stone back to Molikîn, lock it away."

Morik puffed steam from his cup. "The same notion has kicked around in my head, but no. Too many have died to see us stop now."

"How many need to die before there's not enough to get the stone to Helmveline safe? Maybe too many have died for it to be worthwhile already?"

"I refuse to believe that, just as you do."

Solineus chuckled. "So long as we're reading the same story."

"Aye, we've come too far. We kill the witch, *then* I go home."

Solineus nodded. "Ever seen a city of red domes?"

Morik cocked his head. "Can't say I have. What the hells you asking for?"

"Just wonderin'." Solineus sipped his hot brew.

"Tomorrow we'll reach the city of Faldan, no red domes in sight, but we'll have rest and a hot meal."

❦❦❦

Solineus' body felt as if he'd fallen through every last hell when he awoke in the morning. Muscles ached from neck to toe, and more so than painful, they were weak; it was all he could do to get his foot into a stirrup and drag himself into the seat. The ride was slow and sullen, but not so steep, and not so treacherous, as they passed from the snow-line by high sun.

They reached the gates of Faldan as the sun touched the peaks on the western horizon; the city sat nestled in a valley with a sturdy but unimpressive wall and gates on the east-west sides. Unlike the towns and cities he'd seen before, the stone-work showed its age; mortar flaked and cracks from the freeze-thaw cycle went unpatched. Stranger still, not a single guard watched the gates. This flat-out felt unnatural.

And so, they strolled through Faldan without a soul to speak to, and true to the previous standard of hospitality, the Ôshô kept their eyes to the flagstones and paid them no mind unless spoken to. And even then, they tended to walk away fast rather than meet their eyes and answer.

After three salvos Morik got a woman to acknowledge him, and she pointed down the street, with a gesture south. This was the extent of her directions for finding an inn to sleep for the night, but damned if it wasn't good enough. In the end, it was the smell of food which brought them to their destination, and thank the gods a stable stood attached to the inn, or they might've spent another candle looking for stalls and grain.

Whatever one might say about the Ôshô, you couldn't say they didn't know how to keep a room warm. The inn's dining hall blazed with five fires, a fireplace set in each wall and a great round hearth in the middle where gray-haired men and women sat with feet propped close to the flames, sweat rolling down their foreheads and cheeks as they grumbled or laughed at some tale or another.

Their party claimed three tables, pulling them until their backs were to the walls and surrounding a fireplace. Their server was Ôshôin, easy to tell as he brought their ales and meals with fewer words than you might expect from a priest sworn to silence. The stew was antelope and onions instead of goat, and bits of chunky green floaters he couldn't put a name to.

He sipped. Swallowed. Spicy, but not bad. Then the fire came, and he reached for his ale. "Shittin' hells!" He gasped as he chugged, and folks had a good laugh at his expense. Even the Ôshôin elders sitting around the hearth smiled and slapped their knees; it was the closest thing to friendly he'd seen since setting foot in the city, or he might've been more peevish. "What the hells is in that? A demon?"

"Rôkôu peppers." Morik ladled and sipped, blinking. "Strong peppers at that, must've been a good year."

They finished dinner by the time the sky outside turned black, and he half-expected they'd turn in for the night, but one of the gray hairs at the hearth had other ideas. She was a stick of a woman missing half of her teeth, and she stepped to their table with the server in tow. The man held a glass bowl clutched to his chest, shaped like some sort of helm, and an ale so dark it might be black filled it damned near to the rim.

The old gal raised her arms: "The Giant's Helm to quench this foreigner's giant thirst!"

The server clunked the thing on the table in front of him, ale sloshing over the side. He spoke to Morik in Silone: "This woman shittin' me? I can't drink all that." A small keg could be poured into its hollow shell.

And Morik laughed, slapping his back. "No. Stand, take a drink, then pass it around the room. It is good luck if the Giant's Helm is drained before it is set back on a table. Better luck if the man who starts the drinking finishes it."

Everyone in the room stood with him, and several folks clapped in unison, and others hooted and hollered. Five newcomers to the tavern took up the clapping soon as they entered; they were the lucky bastards, timing free ale. He tested his grip then lifted it above his head. "The Giant's

Helm!" And he took as big a drink as he dared, ale pouring down his chin to soak his cloak. He handed it to Morik and joined in the clapping.

The further the Helm traveled the more folks clapped, and soon the tavern rocked with stomping feet. The Helm circled the room once, and the whole of the room let loose with the bellow of "Two!" when he drank a second time, then "Three." Every turn around the room, every clap, every cheer, lifted a weight from his soul. Caught up in something frivolous, the cares of the living and the dead faded, his aching muscles eased, and by the time the Helm returned for his fifth drink maybe half a mug remained. He breathed deep and exhaled, the room in an uproar, chanting for him to "drain the Giant's Helm." He hefted it high above his head before bringing it to his lips, and he quaffed the warm ale's final drop to the cheers of the crowd.

When he sat the Helm on the table in victory, he lowered his eyes to meet Seblêsu's smile.

The Twins dropped to his hips in a flicker, and while half the room still cheered, the other half put hands to hilts, or leveled crossbows at their table.

To a man the Helmveliners stood with hands to the ready as the room's joy faded into a tense silence. Solineus put his hands to the table, ready to flip its planks for cover, but the priestess raised her hand.

"Hold your weapons." She strolled to his table, dragging a chair to plop straight across from him. She eased herself into the seat. "A gentleman would've saved a lady a drink."

Solineus chuckled; whether it was alcohol induced or exasperation, he couldn't say. "You weren't invited."

"A guest is a guest, invited or no. A polite host would sit."

He glanced down the line of Helmveliners. "A polite guest would quit pointing bolts at the host." He sat, hands resting on the table in front of him. The Helmveliners followed suit, Morik last.

She wiggled her fingers at her men, and crossbows dipped. "I didn't expect to see you again."

"Server! An ale for my guest." The boy trotted to the bar and Solineus returned his gaze to her cool stare. "No doubt you expected me dead."

She shook her head, lips pursed. "I expected you to get my message and head home, wherever that may be."

"You have something which belongs to Helmveline."

"Do I? I might suggest it belongs to the Foundations, a holy relic of all the people. I left you everything needed for the Ironwing's posterity… even the rubs so scholars could read that which you lost, but it wasn't enough for you."

"Seven good lives you ended—"

"I? I didn't kill them."

"You deny the quarrel which took Tanzareu's life? The avalanche?"

"You forced me to defend myself, the guilt lies on your head not mine. I wanted no one's life to end."

"And your people who died trying to take other half of the coin—"

"No, no! Do not put those souls at my feet. I already had

what I needed."

Morik scoffed. "The Gold Masks were yours."

The server handed Seblêsu an ale with a shaking hand. She took it and drank, grip steady to not spill a drop. "No indeed! They were not. More hands than mine and yours want Hîmr's Coin."

Solineus shook his head. "It matters not. I want the other half of Hîmr's Coin, and if I have to kill you to get it, it'll be done."

She sighed, leaned back in her seat. "I've shown you great deference in not killing you so far… You are favored by the gods, Survivor of Hîmr's Breath, killing you would be ill-luck. All I ask is for you to leave me be. Please."

She sipped her ale, and damned if Solineus didn't believe her: If he let her go, there would be no more violence. But this presented a problem. He leaned back in his seat and brought a mug of ale to his lips for a flicker to think. "Let us say you are right, part-wise anyhow, and we share the blame for the dead at our feet. It doesn't change one key element."

"That I stole the Waystone? Humiliated you? What is it?" She laughed.

And when her humor faded, he spoke: "What you are doing is wrongheaded. My people gave chase to the gods, and it's because of this that we were driven from our homes, into war with the Hundred Nations, until only thousands survived a journey to the Roemhien Pass."

She stared at him as he drank, her eyes shifting to solemnity. For a moment he held hope. "I believe you mean your words. Hîmr favored you—"

"Hîmr didn't favor me one *spit.* I got lucky. If Hîmr is alive, and it's an if as big as the Giant's Helm... the games gods play aren't for mortals to survive."

"You felt his breath just as I did."

"An elemental. Nothing more."

She studied him and recognized his lie. "No, you too believe he lives... I'd say you know it, though I know not how."

"Leave sleeping gods to their immortal dreams. You won't like them when they're awake."

She sighed and drained her mug. "I can no more deny my destiny than you yours. I apologize for that, because I truly wish we could be friends."

He nodded. "I am sorry too." His heart raced with decisions needing to be made, to fight or stand down, and either might mean dying.

She stood, a sweeping gesture to him and all the Helmveliners. "It would be ill-mannered for either of us to kill the other here and now, might we agree upon that?"

He nodded. "Think on my words. Heed them. Please."

She bowed, a graceful gesture accompanied by a sweet smile. "I will, and you think on mine."

She turned and strolled through the front doors, and two dozen men filed into the star-lit night behind her.

Solineus kicked his feet onto the table, a whistling exhale as his fingers drummed his mug and casual conversation returned to the room. Though no doubt most spoke of them and their kerfuffle. "That's the politest person I ever did want to strangle."

Morik turned to him with a grin and grunt. "So that's it? We should've killed her."

He replied in Silone. "I'm drunk and yesterday you pulled me from a pile of snow, ain't no way in the hells I was gonna pick a fight." No lie. Despite the spin the ale brought to his head, his muscles were stiff and sore.

"And if she handed the shittin' coin over?"

Solineus laughed and raised his hand to summon the server. "I'd kiss her hand and say thank you."

The Kingdomer shook his head. "And you don't think she's gonna try to kill us?"

"Nope! I reckon she'll give us the same chance to think as we're giving her. Then, when we're all someplace far from this place, we'll try to kill each other then."

Morik snorted as ale arrived. "And until then?"

Solineus stood, raising his mug in salute to every Helmveliner, then to every other man and woman in the tavern. "We honor those who've fallen before us… And drink! To peace!"

Ôshôins throughout the hall raised mugs and cheered as if they'd all been friends the whole of their lives, but Solineus held no doubt two or three would carry whispers to Seblêsu's ears.

Morik stood, foaming ale draining down his beard as he spoke. "May we not greet our ancestors in heaven until such time as we've put our worldly work behind us!" Mugs raised, and Morik pulled a silver coin from his pouch and hefted it toward the bar; a nimble hand snagged the treasure from the air. "Tavernkeep! Fill the Giant's Helm!" And the hall thundered its approval, mugs pounding tables and feet tromping and stomping.

Turned out Ôshôins were a pleasant ruckus waiting to happen, all you needed to do was give them a life-and-death show and get them drunk.

Eleven

Dark Waters

She came, she came,
the tongue tying name twisting around the Dame.
The Fire, the Liar, the self-same Desire.
If only you could gaze into your own eyes
and see the truth of your soul, the bowl, the lull, the bull,
the horns forlorn and hammered bent.
Bunny? Funny.

—*Tomes of the Touched*

The morning arrived with Solineus in a bed, half his gear still on, and suffering a hangover like nothing he could remember. He lay on his back staring at the ceiling as the world expanded and shrunk with every beat of his heart and throb of his skull. His voice came as a croak: "Son of a godsdamned holy hell…"

He rolled and damned near tumbled from bed, but his arm braced against the floor to keep him from spinning to the planks. For a flicker he figured he'd vomit, but the sensation passed. He closed his eyes and breathed deep before dragging himself to his feet. He stumbled to the door for support, straightened his armor, and ran fingers through his hair before stepping into the hall with ginger steps.

Voices caught his ear and he made his way to the stairs: A challenge which felt greater than climbing down Yôgul's Fall right this flicker. He took the rail and did his best to play off his lumbering stride as a casual saunter. Bodies littered the room, but they were no more dead than he was, and Morik sat in the same seat as last night with a breakfast of some sort of porridge in front of him.

Solineus approached. "Did you sleep in that gods-damned chair last night?"

A weak chuckle. "May as well have for all the good a spinning bed did me."

A young girl brought him a bowl and spoon, then ladled tan goop; the smell of boiled oat headed straight down his nostrils to make his gut grumble. He plopped in his seat and shoved the bowl as far from his nose as he could reach. He spoke in Silone so not a soul other than Morik would understand. "Any word on the priestess?"

"She's yet to leave the city, unless she tunneled out."

"And seeing as your people're renowned for hidden caves and tunnels?"

Morik's spoonful of porridge bubbled at his lip as he chortled. "Your guess is good as mine. All I know, she didn't leave by no gate we can watch."

"She should've drank with us last night, then we'd know she didn't leave, leastwise not without a pounding head."

"Truth." Morik pulled out Tanzarêu's map of the local mountains and spread it on the table. "Here we are, and here's the nearest known entrance to them caves. It's a long route underground to the Barren Mirror. There's only one godsdamned road to get there, and it's a winding bastard. They leave before us, they'll have the rooster's pick of where to ambush us."

"Why bother? They've got numbers, we can't touch 'em."

"You. You're why she'd bother, he who is favored by Hîmr is a threat. Trouble is, say we leave before her, what the hells good does it do? She'd know we're ahead of her and be prepared."

"This is s'posed to be helpful? We've known our shot is piss poor for a while now."

"Got me to thinkin', the only way to win is for her to think we're behind her, but instead we're ahead of her. I looked at the map last night, and this little jig-squiggle right here."

Solineus glanced, but like so many scrawls on the Huntress' vellum, he didn't know it from a rune-letter. "What the hells is it?"

"Exactly."

A gray-haired man stumbled into the table; no doubt his head pounded as bad as anyone's. He eyeballed Solineus' bowl. "If you aren't gonna eat that?"

Solineus chuckled. "It is yours, friend."

"Much obliged." The man lifted the bowl and slurped, glanced at the map where Morik's finger lingered. "What are you boys whispering about? Erenfol village ain't there no more."

Solineus looked at the map. "There isn't a village marked…"

The old man scoffed and brushed Morik's finger away, tapped the squiggle. "Erenfol's walking well, right there."

Morik's chin rose with a snap. "A walking well? You're sure?"

"I trapped those mountains for as long as you been alive, since the village were still there. And I know my symbols, youngster. You should too." He laughed and strolled from the table.

"What the hells is a walking-well?"

Morik stared at the map, spoke in Silone. "If that old man's right, we want to know she's left before us. Walking wells are rare… instead of digging for water, some villages build entries leading to underground reservoirs or streams, carrying buckets for water."

"You're saying?"

"This walking-well could be right on top of where we need to be. At least close."

It sounded too good, too easy. "Or it might not be connected at all."

Morik rolled the map. "Got a plan better than a suicidal ambush? If you don't, I think this is the best shot we're gonna get."

Solineus rubbed his throbbing eyes. "How much time would it save us?"

Morik sighed, tugged a brass ring in his beard. "Can't say for sure, but I'd say three days. Not including our getting lost in the caves."

Solineus smirked. "You said Kingdomers don't get lost."

"Only when we know where we're going. No matter how deep, I'll get you out again."

"We use this walking well, how do we make your plan work?"

"We wait for word of her leaving, give her a full day's lead, day and a half maybe, in case we're watched. She'll leave men in ambush behind or she won't… either way, we aren't coming her way. With luck, we make the river and figure where she's going before she gets there."

"And we kill her."

"We take the stone. Living or dying is her choice."

Solineus yawned, his head splitting with pain. "I reckon it's the best we got."

❮❃❃❃❯

The road to Erenfol was more bare rocks than the brambles and brush Solineus expected, and in sections you could still find wagon ruts worn into the limestone. The village must've supported a fair amount of trade, he figured, but of what commodity he didn't guess even after they arrived. The foundations and scattered walls of maybe twenty buildings stood on the edge of a valley without a sign of a nearby mine as he expected. The rock, stone, and scattered patches of soil weren't going to support a crop he knew of.

Morik scanned the area. "I'd wager they were scrapers."

"What the hells is a scraper?"

"Miners always look to strike it rich, but it's often a fool's play. So, folks travel about scraping scree and loose rock and cart it off to a smelter. If they find an area with Infused Ore, they'll set camp and scrape out the area until it don't make them a living no more. Been known to take out hillsides."

"Infused ores, like Ikoruv?"

"Aye, don't take more'n a pebble's weight of Ikoruv to feed a family for a month… a year. A lucky scraper won't get rich often, but they do a fine job of feedin' themselves. When they work together in villages, they scrape larger areas and share the profits. Scrape up some Ermôlên or Ofdôlus! and they might feed the village a year."

"I wouldn't know these ores from dirt. The walking well, likely closer to the town or the area they scraped?"

"Once you see Lislinêum you'll never forget it. You'd think the walking well would be close to town, half-candle's walk at most I'd wager. Unlikely a scraper village would have an aqueduct or pipes." He shouted to his men: "Spread out, search the region."

Solineus trailed beside Morik and two Helmveliners with crossbows. Rain, snow, winds, grit, they'd all done their work to destroy or conceal any signs of a trail leading from the ruins. "They wouldn't fill the entrance?"

"Doubtful. Apt to be a natural entrance, they would've chosen the area to build because of the river, once they found ore."

Solineus turned up the side of the mountain above the village for a better view and the others followed. “Rock face yonder looks like it’s been taken to bare rock… same over there. Things don’t grow so well where the villagers scraped.”

“Reckon so.”

A water worn gulley cut through the stone from on mountain high, just to their west, a runoff leading into thick brambles. He pointed. “Rains wash down the mountain there, but no erosion coming out of them bushes.”

Morik whistled. “We Helmveliners have a saying: Sometimes it takes more than a keen eye to see the truth.” He waved an arm over his head. “Clear these bushes! And I wager we find our walking well.

The brambles weren’t eager to give up their turf, with roots digging deep into rocky crevasses and thorns long as a puma’s tooth; strong and sharp enough to sink straight through their heavy soled boots, not a man came away without cuts, scratches, and punctures. Blades struggled to cut the wiry, interwoven mess, even Latcu, so they were reduced to pulling tight and cutting sections at a time. Even then, it was so overgrown they damned near had to clear the whole area just to make a single path.

Solineus was damned happy when he spotted the black crack leading into the mountain’s belly; if they’d found nothing, it would’ve been time, sweat, and blood ill spent.

“Hole’s too small for Ôgrihîn.” Morik stood staring at the fissure. Chiseled steps led into the darkness, roughhewn and uneven, but nothing to fear. "Still, I feel as a hare wandering into the fox's den."

"After a candle clearing the damned thing, if there were anything there, I'd think it would've bit us by now." One thing for certain, with those thorny bushes in the way, this wasn't the route Seblêsu took the Waystone. "All this work, it'd be silly to change our minds now."

"Horse-masters remain here, and if we don't come back in five days or so, you head home and let the Ironwing know where we died and why." Morik turned his gaze on him. "It's Dark Waters and their crossbows I'm worried about. By all means, the favored of Hîmr should go first."

Seblêsu predicted their moves like an experienced hunter, from the Temple of Arumbor to the Red Whistle Tavern. To hope they were a step ahead now felt optimistic, but there was no godsdamned way she knew about this walking well. Was there?

A Helmveliner handed him a lit torch with a grin.

The Twins dropped to his waist and he listened to the Sister's quiet murmur before taking the torch and putting foot to the stairs into the world's mouth. He counted fifty-three steps before touching bottom, but heard the gentle, gurgling flow of water by the time he was half-way down. But once there, he still couldn't see the stream with the meager torch light. His heart thundered; he was a target with a bulls-eye beacon in his hand.

He breathed deep. The mountain air above was dry, down here it was heavy, dank, and cool. He held his torch out; blackness in every direction except for the cavern's wall he'd descended.

"Well, you aren't dead yet." Morik followed him, his fire casting a light further than Solineus'.

The bastard held a lantern with a mirror throwing a beam of light so far that the stream was visible. "You son of a bitch." Helmveliners laughed, half of the bastards carrying similar lanterns. He dropped his torch and stomped on it; thought better of leaving it lay and stuffed it in his pack. "You could have gotten me killed."

Morik grinned with those big teeth. "The hole didn't smell of animal shit nor rot… you were plenty safe."

"Says you." Solineus strode to the stream, narrow enough to jump over and shallow enough his ankles would stay dry if he took a stroll. "Not much of a river."

"Truth. If it don't get bigger downstream we're way off our mark."

Solineus appreciated following this stream through the winding dark, figuring his brain would need addled to get lost, plus, water wouldn't circle around itself. But along the way something else clicked. "If there's a thunderstorm with heavy rains above, what happens down here?"

Morik grunted. "Our trip would get a whole lot faster and wetter. But don't worry none, this time of year there won't be heavy rains in these stretches of the Foundations. Forests to the southeast'll be getting the floods."

Solineus traipsed on, putting faith in the Kingdomer's words to relax. All the while as they walked the stream swelled, fed by small flows slipping from cracks or small tunnels, and in a few locations, they found standing water, fed by springs he guessed. The caves here were bland not beautiful, if not for the water and the bats, it'd be as boring as the tundra, albeit a hells of a lot more comfortable. The rock formations were dull, damned near void of sparkling mineral or character. Boring brown and gritty rock.

Time and distance lost meaning in this hole, so he did his best to annoy the hells out of Morik. "How long and how far?"

"Half a horizon and a few wicks from a full candle since last you asked."

"What direction we facing?"

"South by southeast."

Time for a new challenge. "How deep are we?"

"Ten poles, give or take."

Solineus chuckled, knowing damned well the man wanted to turn and punch him. "Are you making that up? How do you know that?"

Morik snorted. "How *don't* you know it? I ain't sure how you and your people survive, so blind to where you are in the world."

Their stream grew until it was a pole across, but it never swelled into what he'd title a river. However, it did flow into one. The stream's tunnel entered a cavern so wide they couldn't see the far wall, but its ceiling was low enough at points he feared knocking his head.

A quarter horizon later the cavern ballooned to heights he couldn't see, and a hundred strides after, a pillar of stone struck from floor to ceiling, the water shifting their direction to flow around its jagged head; set in the opposite bank, a dried stream bed where once the waters would've split. Maybe still did split, with heavy rains washing from the mountains.

Solineus' eyes plied the darkness, following the streaks of light the lanterns threw. "Think this is it?"

Morik strolled ahead, shining his lantern at the river's flow. Fifty strides wide and gods knew how deep, the river's dark waters flowed until the ceiling was only a couple of feet from the current. Solineus hoped to the Seven Heavens Morik didn't expect him to crawl or swim into that hole.

"This's what the crazy bastards look for… entries into the darkest depths of the world, where Hîmr fled to die." He stepped to the rivers sharp edge and reached to shine his light. Several dark shadows hugged the ground. "Shits. Their boats. We're on the wrong side of the river."

"Godsdamn… At least we know they haven't gone nowhere. Backtrack the river?" He'd crossed too many rivers and didn't look forward to fording one that could sweep him into an unknown abyss.

"We don't know shit from pudding. Better off we sit and wait, with our arbalests we might be able to drop the woman."

Solineus paced. "I don't like it, too much to chance."

Morik grunted. "Then you swim your ass across and kill them! There might be a hundred men marching down that river. Even if she left an ambush behind, she's a cautious woman and she knows how many we are. Most likely she'll keep axes enough by her side to slaughter us, and no doubt enough to fend us off. We won't survive her head on."

"If you miss her, she's gone."

"We miss her from this side, at least we live." He stomped to Solineus' face. "We'll be in pitch black and they'll be carrying lanterns. The range is good."

"Say you kill her, what keeps another from picking it up?"

"Nothing. In truth, I doubt we stop them. But. Say *you're* right, Hîmr *is* alive, and it's a nasty thing stirring up gods... Every one of the bastards we kill is one less soul with a chance of finding him."

"I still don't like it." He turned a circle. "If by some chance they get over to this side, we're trapped."

Morik turned his lantern to the wall of stone, then flipped the beam higher. "There's a ledge there. We can climb and hide if needs be."

Solineus sighed. "I'm still going to see if there's a route across the river."

Morik grunted and held out his lantern. "Waste your time how you like, just don't go getting yourself killed."

❊❊❊

The best Solineus found upriver was a narrow stretch of rapids he might be able to jump across, but the Kingdomers with their short legs were having nothing to do with his idea.

They climbed to the ledge and found a hidden alcove with a circle of stones, where miners or explorers or who the hells knew who once built a fire, as they found a circle of rocks and charred sticks. They tied off ropes from the top to hasten their climb if things went sour.

After that, they sat around in the pitch black, lighting a lantern only to eat, drink, or relieve themselves by the wall. The dark was absolute and unnerving after a time, although the Kingdomers didn't gripe like he did. Maybe their sense of where they were in the world kept them sane in a universe that looked the same whether your eyes were closed or open.

It was a relief when the voices came, and as lanterns lit the opposite side of the river, he wanted to thank them for bringing light, a point of reference for his eyes in this oblivion. He heard men shuffle next to him, and knew they shouldered their arbalests.

Seblêsu's voice rang clear through the cavern. "We should stop here and pray to Sanzumôk the Riven Flow, and praise Hîmr for bringing us this far." Forty or more men kneeled in the lantern light and their voices rose in a deep chant reminiscent of the Mountain Song, only with hollow, contained echoes, rather than the reflections of open valleys.

Shittin' me? Outdoors they'd be in range, but in this dark and a ceiling overhead, he didn't know if they'd get enough loft to their bolts. They'd need wait for them to move further down river. Damnable coincidence, or... His hands strayed to the Twins and they roared in his ears. He whispered, "Something's wrong." He stood, slipping the blades from their sheaths.

Blinding Light.

The Twins screamed, and by the time his eyes adjusted black cloaks with axes swept into them.

Helmveliners fell in the onslaught, cut down without more of a chance to defend themselves than to raise their crossbows before their faces. The Twins, on the other hand, sang for blood.

The Sister sheered an ax-head before taking the man's head, and the Brother struck through another's breastplate until the bastard's chest rammed the hilt. Solineus braced his feet and slid with the impact, then kicked the dying man away. Morik put a bolt through one man and hooked his arbalest to pull his ax, but several others lay dead or dying.

Morik bellowed, "The ledge!"

Helmveliners backed toward the wall with shields and swords and axes fighting off the enemy in a clamor of steel; Solineus found himself lonely and decided to make new acquaintances. He cut the first Dark Water he reached in half as the man pounded a Helmveliner shield with his hammer, and the second lost his head. But it was damned hard getting close to them… One ran and he chased him down, splitting him from the back of his neck to hip, but in the time it took, two more Helmveliners fell. He screamed and went after another, then another as that one fled. Men died all around him, but no one dared face him.

Either they were frightened, or they didn't want the Favored of Hîmr dead.

The Sister reached a Dark Water spine and the man dropped; he turned to face a dozen men in black robes, swords outstretched. Behind him, Morik and three Helmveliners stood their ground with him. "Climb!"

He glanced side to side; to a man they watched him, but not a one made a move to rush him. Sheer numbers would win the battle, but no one wanted to die in victory.

"We're at the top."

Solineus stood straight, blades dancing a slow figure eight before he reached back, grabbing a rope and twining it several times around his forearm before gripping it along with the Sister. "Pull me up!"

His feet lifted from the ground in a split flicker; awkward as rising from the Twelve Hells as he tried his damnedest to walk up the cliff instead of bounce from its face. A man charged and he ran his feet up the wall, damned near flipping upside down, but he gained control to deflect the attack.

He scrambled and clunked the wall, out of reach unless... Several more men arrived, and these carried crossbows. "Faster!" Bruised and sore, maybe bleeding, strong hands grabbed his arm and pulled his beleaguered body over the upper edge as quarrels clinked the stone behind them.

He lay panting until he caught his breath, then pushed backwards out of view of the crossbowmen below. With a turn of his head he still had a view of across the river. Black robes sauntered to the boats in the lantern light, infuriating him even as he sheathed the Twins. "I hope the Dark Waters burn your lungs as you drown in them!"

A shadow stood straight, and he imagined Seblêsu smiled. She was victorious. She deserved it. "I hope you live long with the favor of the Foundations."

Morik snorted. "That woman would apologize for the goat being undercooked even as she poisoned it."

"You realize I knew where you were all the time, the stone works both ways."

Solineus slumped, then chuckled, wishing the Huntress were still alive so he could yell at her. "No, we were told the opposite."

"So I gathered from your ambush."

He watched as men drug boats to the water and her shadow climbed aboard. "One favor."

"Indeed?"

"Think on what I said. If you find Hîmr… Whatever it is you plan, don't."

"To honor your bringing me the stone, I will think on it, but my faith is pure. Hîmr will reward me and my people, and someday the Storm-Eye will rise again." Her boat pushed off into the current. "Goodbye, barbarian. Perhaps we will meet again in another lifetime."

She disappeared into the black carried by dark waters, and more boats with more men followed, and soon their fires disappeared.

Not so the men below. The Light faded but stood replaced by lanterns. These bastards weren't going to float down the dark waters until Solineus and the Helmveliners were dead, or they were shoved dead into them.

❴❃❃❃❵

They were five men against gods knew how many and treed like raccoons, except their tree was ancient stone. Solineus named their hiding hole Castle Ledge, seeing as they were under siege. Seblêsu and her boat floated away two days before, and somehow this little truth angered him more than the fact he'd be dead soon if they didn't cobble their way out of this mess.

The climb to reach them was a good thirty feet, and if more than two men at a time could reach them, it'd still be suicide. Flip that coin, and the roles reversed; might as well jump headfirst to their deaths than climb down to their waiting arms. Solineus rubbed his temples, popped the bung on his canteen and sipped. In time they'd thirst to death with a river no more than twenty strides away. He decided then that he never did like irony.

He crawled to Morik's side and spoke in Silone. "You got our escape reckoned?"

"I throw you and them swords over that there cliff and you kill them all. Don't get much easier than that."

Two of the other Helmveliners slept, the third sat with his chin against his chest, ignoring them. They all needed rest, food, and water. And oil. For the time being their enemy shined a light their way, but if the time came they needed their own fire, they'd run out of light sooner than he liked. "We give them Hîmr's Coin, they might just go away."

"Or, figuring we'd give chase, they'd wait us out and kill us anyhow."

Solineus grunted. "A fist of stonebreakers would be handy."

Morik chortled. "Aye. I'd take my chances with 'em about now."

Solineus stood and walked the ledge and alcove, the light from the priests' mirrored lantern faint. Hard to imagine a better defensible position without maybe building a little wall. Except of course if he'd designed it, he would've put in a back door, and maybe left more good-sized rocks to bash some heads. He wandered over to a stack of blackened stones used as a fire pit in the past; they weren't the first people to use this spot, and his mind often wandered to who the hells bothered to climb to this spot before and why. He clutched a stone and hefted it into the air, then walked back to Morik to sit.

"How far away you think that river is?"

"Further than you can jump. Why?"

"Think you can put a quarrel in that lantern they got shining up at us?"

He chuckled. "Aye, if they don't put one in me first."

"Let's have some fun, wake your boys."

The plan was cold blooded, but there was a reason snakes survived in the dark holes of the world.

With five arbalests and scores of bolts, the enemy kept their distance in the dark, away from the lantern shining light toward their high hiding hole. Morik and the other

Helmveliners crept to the dark edges of the ledge where the light didn't shine, crossbows loaded. Morik took two arbalests, while Solineus slunk into the alcove's edge, as close to the river as he could get.

Two deep breaths and he knocked his stone on the wall twice; a twang and a crash; the lantern spun and clattered, and the world went black. Solineus took one step, couching the stone near his shoulder and prepared to throw. He yelled in the Kingdomer tongue: "Go! Go! Go!" A flicker later he chucked the stone and dropped to the floor to make certain he didn't fall from the edge.

A splash as the rock hit the water.

Hollers and shouts as lanterns flared to life and men ran to the river's edge, swaying lights casting an array of dizzying shadows; ten men, maybe a dozen. Sucker fish easy to the bait.

The arbalests sang as soon as the sway of lanterns slowed, and in a flicker men screamed, lanterns clattered to the ground, and one poor bastard's cloak flared into flames with a lantern's oil.

Solineus crawled to Morik's position as arbalests cranked to reload and found one emptied where he'd expected. He fell backward, jammed a toe into the thing's loop and cranked with both hands. But by the time he'd set the damned thing's string, the bastards had carried their wounded from the light. He slipped a bolt into the crossbow's track. They couldn't see the Dark Waters, as the only light were two lanterns and their patches of oil burning on the ground, but they could hear the grunts, groans, and moans.

"Loose."

Bolts flew, three clatters and one satisfying scream.

A man dashed into the light to grab a lantern, and Solineus shoved his crossbow to Morik; a hurried shot, but from the way he fell, Solineus guessed a strike to the leg.

They cranked the arbalests and set bolts, then listened. No way in the hells they'd be stupid enough to get caught in the open again. Pitch dark, but cries and groans echoed. One man figured for sure he was dying, gut shot, and others rushed to tourniquet another's leg. Hells of a challenge tending the wounded in this kind of dark.

Morik breathed next to him. "Think we hit four or five, but don't think we killed a one."

"Perfect." Cold blooded and effective: A wounded man needed tending; a dead man was plain dead. "They've got choices, let their friends die slow, or drag them someplace safe and lit to mend them."

"Or cut their throats."

Solineus grunted. "In that case, they're colder than we are."

They sat silent and listened; within a wick all they could hear was their own breathing and the river's waters. He whispered in Silone: "Thoughts?"

"Your godsdamned plan, but I'd wager they're gone. But not for long. Or might be they wait for us outside."

"I hope they do, doubt they've an idea where we're coming out." He slithered across the floor until his hands found the curl of rope they'd tied off, and he lowered its end over the edge. He gazed toward the river, where a single lantern lay tipped and burning; if he made it there alive, he figured the odds of living to see the sun again were good.

He clung tight and swung his legs over the edge; flickers later he stood crouched at the base. He unslung Morik's shield form his shoulder and hid behind it, then drew the Brother, a *click* as it unseated in the sheath, but he pulled it slow and steady without a noise after. The Twin whispered in his head, nervous? Maybe ready for a fight but sensing nothing? Hard as hell to read a sword's mind. In his head he chuckled at his own foolishness before skulking toward the lantern. He crouched low, shield covering damned near every bit of him, while expecting the twang of a string any flicker.

He stared over the shield and into the black where men would be as he moved into the lantern's light. Slow. Easy. If they were there, they'd have pulled triggers by now… or they waited for everyone to come down from on high. He grabbed the lantern's wire handle and lifted, pointing its beam to where last he'd heard screams and groans.

Emptiness.

He stood and walked with confidence, flicking the light everywhere he might imagine an enemy, knowing Helmveliners couched arbalests in wait of a target, but as he drew close all he saw was a couple packs and streaks of blood from men being drug away. He whistled twice, and within a couple wicks they followed the blood trail until they came to a fork in the tunnel, where their stream led away from the blood trail.

Solineus asked, "Track and kill them?"

Morik scoffed, his only answer as he turned and trotted down the bank of the stream. The stars were in the sky by the time they climbed from the cave and were reunited with horses and the guards left behind. They sheltered in a three-walled building to catch a couple candles of sleep and come morning they'd ride like the hells to stay alive.

Twelve

A Ruined People

Mend your heart or mend your mind,
turn the table and spin in kind.
The string a hair,
a noose tied corpse fly,
buzzing buzzing circling arc
until the thousand eyes fall.
Flat. Dead. Separated head.

—*Tomes of the Touched*

"The good news is, with the woman gone with her piece of the stone, she won't be able to tell folks where we are." Solineus gnawed on jerked goat between scratching at healing scabs and bruises. He wished for a fire to warm his sleep chilled bones, but it wasn't worth the risk.

"We should send a pigeon to Molikîn, Sînhôlar the Ironwing will want to know what has happened."

"Aye. And you should return Hîmr's Coin for safe keeping."

"Me? What, by the Five Earls, will you be doing?"

"I'll be heading west." He pulled the coin from his cloak and handed it to Morik.

The man turned it in his hands before concealing it in an inner pocket. He reached into his pack and pulled out Tanzarêu's maps. "My ass will appreciate your leaving me, but I hope someday your path leads you back to Shuntiskâ." He stretched the map of the Foundations and lay it on the ground, pointed. "There are no red-domed cities in the Foundations, which means your road is a long one. Beyond the Foundations are the Ilû-Strono Plains, no proper cities there in the land of the Ilu, the lion people."

"Ilu-Silvstro? I've heard of them."

"That's one of the big tribes. Tread gently into their lands, they can gut a bison with their bare hands… and their women are big as you are and stronger. But if you manage to become their pain in the ass friend, you should find passage to the cities of the Helebôm in this region."

"What do you know of the Helebôm?"

"Nothing but what I've heard. They rule the port cities and host trade with the known world, even Luxuns."

"I've met Luxuns… good people."

Morik perked. "Their hair and skin are as people say?"

Solineus laughed. "Aye, it is."

A wistful looked crossed his face. "I've never seen the great waters, maybe someday, but I do love my mountains. Anyways, if your domed city is further west than the Helebôm you'll be needing something seaworthy."

Solineus stared at the map. "Any Teks I need worry about?"

"If you hit this here—"he pointed to a river with cliff-marks on either side"—you've found the Orstân Rift, beyond is held by the Hundred Nations. Your bigger worry will be getting out of the Foundations alive if the Dark Waters look for you. They'll expect you to deliver word of the stone to the Foundations, so I'd avoid the homes of kings. And no griffon cloak."

"What if I leave the mountains?"

Morik shook his head. "Teks to the north, and not gentle ones like you've known." He grinned and tugged his beard. "South? That'll take you out of your way and you're as apt to get eaten as make it alive. Best to stay in the Foundations. I know a smith here, in Holvin Dô-ar." He tapped a hammer-and-fire symbol maybe a hundred horizons from the walking-well where they sat and traced the roads he should travel. "Âemêsu was born on the face of Shuntiskâ and raised in Molikîn. I trust her to keep you and your secrets safe."

Solineus knew the man well enough to recognize the cogs in his head aligning. "This Âemêsu might get me west?"

"Maybe… I will bypass Shînvedorn, make way to Elimmor. I'll send pigeons out every which way saying you're continuing to deliver the rubs to the kings, that might ease my path some. When you reach Holvin Dô-ar you sit tight until I reach Molikîn. I'll send word that Hîmr's Coin is with the Ironwing. With this known, Âemêsu and the

Forges of Holvin have trade in all directions, she might see you safe and sound once no one hunts you. I'd give that some time to make sure word spread." He rolled the maps and held them out. "You'll need these more than I."

Solineus took the maps. The plan sounded slow for his taste, but he'd get nowhere dead. He had a small pouch of coins, but doubted they see him far. "I'll need dâguts to travel… I know, I'm a pain in the coin purse friend."

Morik laughed as he reached into his pack and handed Solineus a pouch of coins. "Keep that hidden, let any cutpurse steal the one at your waist first. And don't ever tell me how much is in there, getting technical like, it's the Ironwing's treasury anyhow. Still, it might make me cry."

Solineus laughed as he stood and hugged the barrel-chested man, thumping his back with a laugh. "Until we meet again in Shînvedorn."

They saddled the horses and stowed their gear in a matter of wicks, and it was Solineus who departed first. Leaving friends behind, both living and dead, was becoming a bad habit, but he took the advice he'd given Ivin what seemed an eternity ago: He looked forward, not back.

Mountains. Mountains. Mountains. More godsdamned mountains.

He chuckled and patted his gelding's neck, then grumbled. "I should've grabbed a shield." But that'd mean turning around. Heels met ribs and they broke into a trot to ease the temptation to turn.

By midday he found a road he figured was named Pozdonu, if reading Tanzarêu's map right. From here he anticipated the route to Holvin Dô-ar to be straightforward enough, except there was nothing straight about it. A hundred horizons as the pigeon flies took twenty-days by the time the roads twisted and climbed.

The city sat near the eastern border of the Kingdom of Kâmar, with Ôshô to the south and east, and Tûrûrôt to the northeast, although borders flexed here and there depending on which passerby he spoke to.

One thing for certain, even if he tried to get lost, all he'd have to do is ask to have his path corrected; Holvin Dô-ar was renowned for its smithy. The people of Kâmar were friendly and within a sentence asked what a foreigner was doing, so he'd crafted his story around a commission from the Mountain Lord of Shuntiskâ. If he'd thought about it long, he might've concocted some other tale, but once he'd spoken the words they stuck in his head.

Folks jabbered high praise for the craftsmen and their hammers, but not once did a soul prepare him for what he'd see on his arrival.

He rounded his thousandth turn in the past two weeks and rode from beneath the evergreen branches of a copse of firs to find a city clinging to the side of a mountain. He jerked his reins to stop and stare: Half of the city, maybe more, lay in rubble sloughed from the side of the mountain in a heap of crumbled towers and walls. Thousands, maybe tens of thousands died in such a calamity. It took flickers for the trees amid the rubble to register; this was no recent disaster, it'd happened decades before, maybe even further in time. The original road, too, was gone, but a newer road circled the rubble and rose to a gatehouse that'd been added to a section of collapsed wall.

The impression was one of riding to ancient ruins, maybe a part of a civilization the Touched would blabber about in confusions of time and place, but his arrival at the gates opened his eyes to reality; three guards stood watch in armor fashioned from plates, articulated at the joints, and buffed to a blue-gray shine. He'd never seen its like and wondered how ordinary weapons would penetrate such gear without finding the slit of the helmet's visor.

A guard removed his helm to reveal a youthful, shaved face with squinting eyes. "Your business?"

"I seek the smith, Âemêsu of the Helmveline, with a commission from Mountain Lord Morik of Shuntiskâ."

"What sort of commission?"

No one bothered to ask this before, but his tongue worked with a wit faster than his brain. "A shield."

The guard strolled to his side, staring up at him, glanced at his horse and gear, then circled him. "Ikoruv hilts?"

Not a question he expected, the leather must've slipped. "Yes."

The guard raised a hand into a fist and the portcullis ground open. "Welcome to Holvin Dô-ar."

Solineus smiled with a nod. "Appreciate it. Is there an inn I might find a bed at?"

The man's look was stone-eyed. "Inn? No. Head for the Sun Forge."

"Where's that?"

A blink. "Straight ahead."

Solineus gave a curt nod and nudged his mount to walk through the gates. To his left, east, the city disappeared from a cliff, but straight ahead and west buildings still stood. The clop of steel-shod hooves echoed; the city was damned near empty, though he'd learned that Kingdomer towns and cities were often like Istinjoln: Busier beneath the surface. A few folks skittered like bugs from one building to another, but they didn't hold his attention.

A squat building fashioned from white marble stood in front of him, broad and with one set of double doors for an entrance; a dozen or more chimneys at its edges puffed gray smoke into the blue sky, but a golden dome rose from its middle, and from there billowed a white smoke, or perhaps steam, it was difficult to tell.

He dismounted and flipped his reins over a weathered hitching post out front. The doors stood wide open on a pleasant sunny day, and he didn't see a soul until he stepped through. The woman's back was to him as she perused a wall full of books, her hair in a long black braid that stretched to her calves. He cleared his throat.

"Your name?"

"Solineus Mikjehemlut of the Clan Emudar."

That mouthful got the attention he expected. He hoped she wasn't a member of the Dark Water Cult. "You aren't supposed to be here."

"And I'd appreciate it if you kept it quiet."

She smiled before covering her mouth. "What brings a barbarian to Holvin Dô-ar?"

"Âemêsu of Molikîn."

Her brows arched. "Ah! Of course. I must ask, first, do you have Hîmr's Coin with you?"

He laughed. "It was lost, I fear. But I have a rub if you'd like to see."

"I would!" The shock on her face when he pulled the vellum from his cloak suggested she didn't quite trust him. And the fact he placed it in her hands paled her face. "The Storm-Eye be praised… it's like I'm touching history."

"Stare at it all you like, but first get me to Âemêsu."

She giggled. "Of course."

The building was huge, and he followed through several halls, into blazing hot rooms with raging fires, enquiring after the smith until they found her in her study deep in the back of the building. She answered the door wearing a heavy leather apron which sported a hundred charred blotches, her hair a silver-gray and pulled into a tight tail. Her visage was of a pissy old woman with a vinegar-scowl attitude.

"Markîk's curse, what do you want?"

His guide's voice was smug and self-pleased. "This is Solineus Mikjehemlut… of the Clan?"

"Emudar."

"Yes, Emudar."

The smith's scowl went flat, and her eyes flicked to meet his. "What, by the Five Earls, would you want with me?"

"Morik of Shuntiskâ said you might be able to assist me."

"Inside. You close the door and be off."

He stepped inside and she gestured to a chair. The room was piled full of stuff surrounding a single bed. Books, slat-crates filled with slags of metal, four tables, a dozen chairs (all but the one in which he took a seat covered in clothing tossed at random) and a statue of a black cat. Except it turned out the cat was alive and fond of his lap. It leaped onto his legs and curled with a purr the flicker his ass hit the wicker.

"You're a blazing hot ingot, and this here city has rules."

"I've no idea what you mean."

She stared at him as if to judge, then shoved junk from a second chair on to the floor so she could sit. "The Sun Forge sits in Holvin Dô-ar, and Holvin Dô-ar sits in the Kingdom of Kâmar, but smiths from the breadth of the Foundations come here to learn and create. This means no ingots heated by the politics of kings."

He cocked his head, figuring what the hells she spoke of. "The Sun Forge is neutral ground."

"Yes."

"Then I am unwelcome? Because I claimed Hîmr's Coin?"

"Any man must have a claim to be welcome to the Sun Forge. You, more so than most."

"A claim?"

"A reason to visit."

He unsheathed the Sister and held out the blade. "Is this reason?"

The woman blanched, her fingers reaching out before pulling back. "Spirit-blade?"

"Indeed."

She exhaled a deep breath. "While fascinating… No, you must either be a recognized smith or have something you wish made."

He chuckled. "Morik claims I need a shield."

She grinned. "You may have a shield forged anywhere."

"Morik claimed I can trust you… can I?" She nodded with a palm up gesture. "He carries the coin back to Molikîn as I speak, but the Dark Waters believe I have it. He figured I'd be safe here for a time, until he can spread word that the Ironwing holds the coin. Tell me what I need to find the good graces of the Sun Forge."

"Pigeons spoke of the barbarian hero carrying the coin through the Foundations?"

"A ruse."

She nodded, sighed again. "If you need a shield, you need a shield. It just can't be an ordinary shield to be made anywhere."

"A friend of mine has a shield which can stop Latcu arrows."

She blinked then stared long and hard. "That… that is a feat." She scratched her head. "This I cannot do. How many dâguts do you have?"

He tossed her his pouch of coins and she didn't bother to look inside; her breath puffed. "The Sun Forge doesn't come with silver and a few specks of gold. Even if I worked free… the Forge demands its pay."

"How much?"

"Much."

"More than the Ironwing would owe the man who brought him Hîmr's Coin? Send him a pigeon with your price."

She leaned back in her chair. "You've met the Ironwing in person?"

"Twice, at the Third Throne."

Her smile meant she was impressed. "*Tûmoshu melor.* In the young tongue, a Singing Shield. The Ironwing can afford it, and the Sun Forge won't refuse this profit. If his pigeon returns a treasury note."

"It will." He hoped his confidence would pay off as he locked eyes with the woman and petted the cat.

"I will put in the necessary reacquisitions, and *if* the Ironwing sees fit… a week maybe to receive the treasury writ… in a month we might start work on your Singing Shield."

Whatever the hells that is. "I would be honored."

She laughed. "As you should be. I must be back to work… but I'll have the girl prepare a room for your stay, and later we will visit the pigeon-master."

She stood and opened the door but glanced back. "Tongs has taken a liking to you."

He assumed this was the cat's name. "Indeed. A fine feline, but he won't let me get up." She laughed as the door closed behind her, but he wasn't lying; Tong hissed when he tried to stand, then purred as soon as he relaxed. He rubbed the cat's head between the ears. "You do realize I outweigh you about ten to one? And I'm wearing armor?" He snorted as the cat closed its eyes for a doze and kneaded his cloak.

What the hells, he didn't have no place to go anyhow. "Fought my way thousands of horizons just be beaten by a five-brick pussy cat." He leaned back in the chair and closed his eyes; maybe a nap was what he needed anyhow.

Thirteen

Forge the Sun

The terror in the error,
the weather carrying the feather,
dead weight, the dead wait, float what for,
in the forbidden necromantic lore?
Can't say, won't say, shouldn't say,
but I did! Did I? Not yet.
Bloated noses above the waves,
not dead. No, no, alive and hungry.

—*Tomes of the Touched*

"You know of infused ore?"

With King Sînhôlar's treasury writ deposited with the Sun Forge, Solineus' status at the Sun Forge earned him an education. It didn't hurt that Âemêsu and every smith who caught word of the Twins wanted to test their ability to cut a variety of alloys. "I know the words. Something to do with the Elements altering the metal."

"Indeed. What is Ikoruv?"

"Metal." He grinned until she drummed her fingers on the table. "Infused iron?"

"Indeed! Every metal has an infused sibling, so to speak. Ikoruv means 'holy iron' in the ancient tongue, but there's nothing godly about it."

"Then how does it become Ikoruv instead of iron?"

"I suppose the gods could create it." She chortled. "This is one of the great mysteries of my trade. You've heard also of infused gems? Diamonds which heal…"

"Pearls which connect two souls."

Her head cocked. "I never heard of this, but many things are possible. Gems may be found infused, the most powerful by far, while others a lapidary might infuse themselves. One Element. An infused diamond is most often imbued with Life. Not so with metals… they don't heal, they don't bind the dying's soul to their body, they don't prevent the deceased from becoming the Wakened Dead. So, the theory is that they are "infused" by, not with, all the Elements at once, and this creates a metal with unusual properties."

"What metal is Latcu?"

"None. Many assume it's a form of infused diamond, or perhaps infused volcanic glass. Nobody knows."

"So Ikoruv, what makes it so valuable?"

She reached into a box and brought forth a bar of black metal, dropped it onto the table. Then, a chunk of what looked like a black rock, except its flat faces reflected the light with a metallic glint. "Ikoruv in its native form, and one smelted. Both of these will be used in your shield. Steel is iron made hard with carbon, too much carbon and it becomes brittle and breaks. Ikoruv is hard as steel in its natural state, harder even, and it flexes with a more perfect memory of its shape than steel. You want as little carbon as possible in its use."

"And you need the Sun Forge to smelt Ikoruv?"

"It is very difficult to bring a normal forge to a heat to melt Ikoruv, but it can be done in several places throughout the Foundations. But it is with greater effort." She lifted a silvery bar and set it on the table. "This is?"

It felt like a trick question, but he went with the obvious answer expecting to be wrong. "Silver."

"Indeed. And this?" A second silvery bar, but in this case the color held a blood-red tint.

"I'm guessing infused silver?"

"Ofdôlus, yes, known as the 'blood chime'. It is the metal which gives the Singing Shields its name. The Ikoruv gives the shield is strength, Ofdôlus its tint and song." She picked up a dinner knife and rapped the Ikoruv with a clunk, but on striking the Ofdôlus, it was as if a chime had been struck. A perfect low note.

"It's beautiful."

"Forge these two metals into a shield and you have an amazing tool. Protection, indeed! Near indestructible. But they also play their song, and men use them to send messages in battle, or to intimidate the enemy before a fight. But what else would it be?"

He leaned back in his seat with a smile. "Heavy."

"Which is where the third ingredient for your shield comes in." She reached behind her to grab a jar and plopped it on the table.

"An empty jar?"

She flipped it upside down, and a silvery-liquid floated to the base of the jar, which was now the top. "Lislinêum. Infused Mercury. Lighter than air, and when alloyed into your shield, reduces the weight by half. When we have enough Ofdôlus and Lislinêum we will be able to start your shield."

Solineus grabbed the jar, turning it a couple times; floating blobs of shiny silver hovered then rose. "Has anyone ever crafted a water-clock with this stuff?"

She laughed, but then her brows scrunched. "An interesting notion."

"Ivin's shield is lighter than it looks, I'd wager it's an Ikoruv-Lislinêum alloy."

"Ikoruv won't stop Latcu by its lonesome. Someday I would like to see this Warlord's shield."

The infused ores were slow in arriving, so Solineus spent a lot of time getting to know Tongs the cat better and waiting for pigeons from Kinesee and Morik. Three notes from Kinesee, but not a word from Morik; he grew worried for the man as it'd been two months since they parted ways. A week later a shipment of cinnabar, and as he watched Lislinêum float from the reddish mineral thoughts of Morik faded to the back of his mind; Âemêsu had her materials to start the shield and would only need to wait for forge time to get to work.

He should've known better than to get excited; word from Morik arrived before work began. Hîmr's Coin rested safe in the vaults of Molikîn, and Morik was home in Shuntiskâ with his wife and children. His heart at peace with this news, Kinesee's next letter proved a better distraction for his imagination.

Dear Father,

Pigeons have been my distraction these past weeks as we've moved into a new building built in the Roemhien next to the wall, which is taller than me now across most of the gap. Eight towers are planned plus the keep.

The Pigeon-master here is named Zetru, a pretty gal not much taller than Meliu. She is letting me name several baby pigeons, and I thought of calling them after my lost family, but I grew depressed by the notion, in particular after Zetru noted how often young pigeons die, get lost, or otherwise disappear. Therefore, I started naming them all after the irritating Ravinrin boy. Trouble is, I could only come up with so many insulting names involving 'fish'. Still, I strive for new insults every day, and with Zetru's help we've been including Kingdomer names, including Blind Fish.

A hundred people, give or take a hundred depending on which day it is, have taken to camping south of the wall along the pass. Families already hunt to the south and word is several plan expeditions into the dense forests found out of the mountains.

Ivin believes he spotted an Ôgrihîn at a distance the other day; he claims it's twice the size of a Colok. You know more of what that'd mean as I never seen none of the Colok. Ivin said to imagine something with a body the size of a bison, only walking like a man on legs like tree trunks. I tried not to imagine it.

Meliu has disappeared from Ivin's life since we came to the wall, which is good. I adore her, but the eyes she and Ivin make would be bad enough without disturbing talk of the Codex of Sol. Still no clue in the prophecies of why anyone would want me dead.

So! I'm alive.

Your pearl rubber,

Kinesee

Âemêsu invited Solineus to the Sun Forge for the first time the day after Kinesee's latest note winged into the pigeon-master. He wore nothing but his lightest linens as instructed, but kept the Twins on his back. Within a flicker of stepping into the hall he dripped with sweat and his clothes stuck to him.

Âemêsu handed him a canteen and gestured toward the center of the room. A massive cauldron, with feet shaped as the heads of gryphons, and fashioned from some white metal rested dead center in the room. There was no fire he could see, but there was a light as intense as the heat in the room emanating from a structure dangling above the cauldron like a chandelier. Men and women clad in heavy aprons and heavy gloves moved around the room, but no one drew close to the forge.

She pointed to a platform which stood twenty paces from the center. "That there is as close as we get to the Sun Forge unless we need to, and then we wear goggles to block the light. Men have gone blind when drawing too close."

"I'm as close I need to be." He took a drink of water.

She slapped him on the back and led him toward the platform's steps. "Come! Those bars leading from the platform have grooves. We place materials in them and raise our end to dump the metals into the forge to heat." They climbed atop and a man brought her two small crates. She pointed again, to a mirror above the forge; the reflection showed the bottom glowing red. "First it will glow a hundred shades of yellow before turning hundreds of shades of red, before turning a hundred shades of blue. Once blue it would be hotter, much hotter than we need."

"What the hells requires hotter than Ikoruv?"

"A few of the rarest ores."

"What makes it so hot?"

"You remember our conversation about infused gems? The Sun Chandelier holds gemstones, all infused with Elemental Heat. A vestige of the God Wars. No living man knows how to craft another."

Solineus whistled. This was a thing men wouldn't simply kill for, they'd go to war if they could figure out how to move it. No wonder the Kingdoms all agreed to share.

She turned to an assistant. "A half keg of water if you will." She lifted three balls of Ikoruv and placed them in a groove and waited as the man lifted and poured water down a broad pipe. Steam billowed as the water hit the forge, and for the first time he looked up; a golden dome with a hole allowed the steam to escape.

His eyes lowered as the Ikoruv balls rumbled down the chute, and he gazed into the mirror to watch them hit the cauldron's round bottom and rolled in circles, but they turned red within flickers.

"A quarter keg of smelt-water." Water flowed and the Ikoruv disappeared in steam. "Ikoruv is mostly pure to start, but steam can help remove the few impurities which might persist after they're smelted into balls."

When the steam cleared, he watched as the Ikoruv pooled and bubbled into a glowing red mass. "Peculiar in its beauty."

"Indeed! The Sun Forge is art in many ways, masterworks few people will ever see." She lifted a ball of silvery-red metal and tossed it to him; unready, his hand rushed to the catch, but it fell slow until resting in his palm with a gentle landing. And she laughed. "I alloyed the Ofdôlus and Lislinêum yesterday… visitors aren't allowed to witness this procedure. But, if we tried to add the Lislinêum raw, it would turn to gas in the heat required to melt the Ikoruv."

Solineus tossed it back to her, the shimmering ball falling at a feathers pace. "That is impressive."

"Indeed!" She took three alloy balls, each about a quarter the size of the Ikoruv, and rolled them down the chute. They hit the molten Ikoruv and disappeared in splotches of silver that spread to cover the bubbling surface. They stood and stared, but she didn't tell him what they waited for. She turned to the assistant. "It is done. Drain it."

She led him back down the ladder and straight toward the door. "Where does it go?"

"It drains to an underground chamber. Here the masters of the Sun Forge will weigh the material again to make sure the Ironwing will pay right and proper. After, they will bring it to me, and the real work begins."

Solineus drained his canteen in chugs after setting foot outside the Sun Forge, savoring the light breeze traveling the hall. They sat in her chambers for a candle waiting, and he jumped at the knock on her door; he hated to admit how excited he was to see the thing.

A woman at the door handed Âemêsu a disc of metal close to four feet in diameter. She turned to him with a smile and tossed it at him. It came fast with no lack of weight, but it was lighter than he'd imagined. The black Ikoruv weighed a brick at most and was so thin. He grinned at her. "You sure that'll stop anything?"

She snatched it away with pursed lips. "Your head won't dent it, I assure you." She struck the disc with her knuckles and the metal chimed. "The molten metals bond, but—"she flipped the disc, the reverse side a beautiful silvery red—"as you saw in the forge the Ofdôlus alloy shows on one side. I will heat and pound it until its concave. With the black on its face its song will be bass and it will show less damage, with the silver it will be higher, and more beautiful in appearance and tone, but more prone to scratch. It is your choice."

The red-silver tempted him, gorgeous, but such a reflection might get him killed. "Ikoruv on the outer."

"This is the warrior's choice." She grinned. "And the assassin's."

He squinted with a grunt. "I'm no assassin."

I failed at that.

Fourteen

The Low Mountains

Tenor's vibrato from the hawk's beak,
soaring sleek ignoring the vulture's favorite wreak.
Song sung or cursing the blinding sun,
updrafts carry the carrion's uncaring laugh
to the wing-ed ear, beaten back by wings aflap,
the dead man smiles and cares not for smells he makes,
he only wishes to be heard and understood.
Words, words, rotten words,
Words, words, fading from rotten flesh.

—*Tomes of the Touched*

Winter came and did its damnedest to bury the Sun Forge and the city of Holvin Dô-ar, but no snow could stick to that building and its golden dome as fires burned. However, it guaranteed he'd be stuck there until the spring thaw.

Which turned out just fine, as his shield wasn't done by then. Âemêsu worked his shield every day, but split time on multiple projects. No way to hurry perfection, she assured him. One day near spring she presented him with the disc, pounded into a concave shield glorious to behold… then she took it from him. The next step was the polish. And again, perfection couldn't be hurried.

The snows were long gone, grasses grew, and birds sang, by the time she handed him the shield for keeps. And when she did, she grabbed a hammer and pounded at him: Not a mark, let alone a dent, but his shoulder felt the impact the next morning. Despite the pain, he'd determined to leave, but again Âemêsu held other plans.

"A man not of the Sun Forge isn't allowed to travel with our deliveries." She held up a single silver dâgut. "But I can hire you as escort. This is all I can afford, seeing how I worked on your shield for a pittance, but if you hire on, you'll have a safe journey so far as Klondihîk in Barkûsh. It'll slow your pace, but you'll be passing through regions thick with Ôgrihîn… slow is better than dead."

Solineus grumbled and scowled, but snatched the coin from her fingers with a vision of Kinesee's description of the beasts in his head. "A pittance, my ass."

She winked and strolled away, and a week later he rode from Holvin Dô-ar amid a caravan of four wagons and forty warriors. Not a soul offered to tell him what cargo he guarded, and he didn't bother to ask; so long as it wasn't stonebreakers, he was happy to be back in the saddle and riding.

What he discovered in less than a day was that his body was no longer used to a saddle, and he ached for three days before his muscles acclimated. Their route took them east before turning west, then swung them to the city of Dôldên in the Kingdom of Ômkinter. On the surface Dôldên appeared a small, sleepy place with thick black walls and an undersized gatehouse, but its streets bustled with Kingdomers and he learned later that he stood atop one of the largest mining complexes in the Foundations, with hundreds of horizons in tunnels winding beneath the five surrounding mountains. They unloaded nailed-shut crates of goods and loaded boxes that rattled with loose ore. Several guards left and more hired on, disciplined and efficient in every stage.

A two-day stint to hire and resupply before they traveled past the Ômkinter towns of Nîzin, Vêrdan, and Homtok before entering the mountains of the Kingdom of Œrinklîn. Here their primary stop was in the city of Gîgan, but to his mind it was more a fortress. Horizons of massive walls surrounded a mountain valley and a river flowed through its middle before filling Lake Terbemor a hundred horizons to the south. The Œrinklîn people were more standoffish than other kingdoms, more reserved, but till downright jocular compared to the Ôshô.

They spent a week in Gîgan and he suffered a couple hangovers drinking with other guards before he smartened up and turned in early every night. Kingdomers could hold their weight in beer and ale, and he swore they didn't even need to piss as often as he did.

From Gîgan they wound through some of the roughest mountains he'd yet seen, and instead of making their way to mines and towns, riders followed rocky trails into the mountains and brought back mule trains of raw ore. Travel was slow as treacle flowing uphill in the winter, and at some point, he wasn't sure when or where, they'd entered the Kingdom of Danlok. They traveled for weeks and only entered one city, Yusdulên, and only for a night and fresh supplies.

A few days from Yusdulên moods brightened; the terrain changed as they passed the border into Barkush, and they found the roads wider, flatter, and straighter. He learned that Barkûsh meant "low mountains" in the old tongue, but it might as well have meant pleasant. Only the tallest mountains wore snow on their crowns, the ridges and valleys were rolling rather than severe, and everything that wasn't a rock stood covered with grasses sporting flowers on their heads instead of thorns. The sun shone through gauzy clouds, and the rains they met were warm. Other guards nicknamed the region "*Tusfala Emit Mêomet,*" the Land the Gods Smiled Upon.

They rolled past a dozen villages before they reached the city of Klondihîk, which sat on and surrounded the low mountain of the same name. Gleaming white marble walls rose in three tiers before a square keep rose high from atop the peak, where banners of yellow, blue, and green snapped in the winds. From his vantage on first seeing the city, he spotted six roads leading to the eastern gates; he recalled Ivin's tale of the city of Bdein and its wealth and wondered if he'd just found its rival.

From a distance it appeared ideal, but it was also a king's city, a place the Dark Waters would expect to find him. If they still bothered searching for him.

The streets were clean, the people polite, and he'd never before seen so many horses without there being a battle. And some pulled carriages, silk covered, and they even had lanterns built right into them. Minstrels performed on the street corners of the trade district, and as they probed deeper into the city, strings of colorful pennants adorned the streets.

No city could be so perfect all the time. He rode to Junûk's side, the head of the guardsman. "Klondihîk always this festive?"

"Not so far off! But, the Festival of the Righteous Dancer is less than a week away." Righteous Dancer referred to the goddess Insôum, but this was all he knew. "Barkûsh from across the realm will arrive throughout the week, some family of mine own, no doubt."

Wicks later they rolled into a caravansary like he'd never imagined. A full three dozen wagons lined the courtyard, each with Kingdomers crawling over them like ants on honey to haul crates and supplies into three-story warehouses. Opposite the windowless warehouses stood the pretty sibling, three stories as well, but sporting stained-glass windows and flapping banners and pennants. Along its face, a covered boardwalk with two doors leading inside, one gilt in silver, the other gold.

Junûk pointed. "Gold doors are for the merchants, silver for us guards, drivers, and hands. Rooms are at a reasonable price and you'll work hard to find thicker, softer down ticks anywhere."

"I won't be staying long. You're of Barkûsh?"

"I am."

Solineus reached into his cloak and pulled forth a scroll, handing it to the man. "Your king will want this. Deliver it, there might be some small reward."

The man glanced, then slipped it into his pack. "A rub of Hîmr's Coin?"

Solineus grinned. "You knew?"

"There are barbarians in the Foundations, sure, but not many with Ikoruv hilts over their shoulders."

"I wasn't aware the rumors were so specific."

Junûk shrugged. "I will make sure His Highness Tehemdor receives it."

"My thanks. Do you know a city of red domes, somewhere west of here?"

The man cast him a sideways glance. "Red domes. Mulshuhar, or at least it could be. It is said their temples are domed in red-gold."

"Thank you, may the Storm-Eye bring you peace." Solineus nodded and reined his horse to the stables, handing the gelding and Âemêsu's silver dâgut to a stable girl before strolling to the silver-gilt door.

The scent of cedar was heavy in the room, the red-streaked golden wood lining the walls and ceilings, while the floor was flagstones. There were candles until nightfall but still he yawned as he rented a room, and vowed to get to sleep early and awake at first light to ride west, but after he sunk into the comfort of the feather-ticked bed he realized the former would be easy enough, but the latter might be damned near impossible. Dragging himself from this bed might only be accomplished with hunger.

❮❄❄❄❯

He awoke without a clue of what time it was; all he knew was there wasn't a sun. He cursed himself for going to bed too early, clinched his eyes shut, and squirmed into the pillowing cushion of the tick. This was good, real good. He lay there, ignoring the urge to move, and dozed.

Click.

His head raised and his left eye cracked open just enough to gaze at the door. The only light came from the moon and stars through a single window until the door swung open a crack to let in the warm yellow light of a lantern in the hall.

The crack gaped and the door hit the wall as a man stumbled and fell to a knee with a laugh. He reeked of pipe smoke and whiskey, and Solineus didn't recognize him as being from their caravan. A woman laughed and stumbled around the door's frame.

She laughed. "You're too drunk you still pay."

He stood, wobbling, slapping his hips with both hands. "I never get so drunk, woman."

Solineus sat up, cleared his throat. "You've got the wrong room, friend."

The man jumped and belched, and the woman cackled. "You sod! I'm not taking a poke from the both of you."

But the drunkard turned on Solineus. "Get your ass out of my room, barbarian."

Solineus dove for the Twins before the man realized his mistake, but the bastard was quick. Knives flashed and slashed. Solineus caught an arm and spun the man as the other knife caught his ribs, and he kicked the man in the head, before spinning him to slam him into the bed. Slamming him into a pile of cushy pile of feathers wasn't going to do the trick.

He put his weight into an elbow to the back of the man's head before he felt the knife in his side; he whirled and caught the woman's cheek with a backfist before lunging for the Twins. They screamed into his mind as they flicked from their sheaths, and the charging man dropped, split from shoulder to pelvis with a reek.

The woman bolted out the door, and Solineus damned near followed. No, there was no telling if these two had friends. He closed the door and rammed a chair beneath its handle. The hole in his side was small, some sort of push-dagger he guessed, and he stuffed the wound and wrapped a strip of sheet around his midsection (covering both the light gash and puncture) before throwing on his breastplate, mail, and helm.

He wore everything he owned as he left the room, prepared to fight or run, with his shield in one hand and the Sister in the other. The lantern's soft glow revealed no one in the hall, so he stepped back into his room and barred the door again. He stepped to the window and pushed, slipped through, and dropped to the street in a crouch.

Moon and stars were his only guide in a city he didn't know from an ant hill's maze. A blur whizzed past his head and thunked the wall, and he ran without a clue where the missile had come from. Footsteps behind him.

He slid around a corner and ducked behind a rain barrel. Two men sprinting didn't see him. The first lost both of his legs, the other his head, and the Sister shrieked her glee between his ears. The no-legged man managed a single scream before the Latcu pierced his throat.

He stood panting over their carcasses, but within flickers there were shouts and a whistle blowing, the voices coming his way. He couldn't make out what they said, but he didn't doubt who they were: city guard. He was a barbarian who'd just killed three men, and for all he knew the king himself had ordered his death.

"Shits." He ran. He didn't know where he was or where to go, but running was the only thing which made sense. He turned and turned and turned, then slowed, spotting a small wagon sitting outside a shop not far away. He moseyed its way and glanced at the wagon's bed: nothing but a few scraps of hay.

Wide open to the sky and stars, whether assassins or guards walked past, he was plain to see. He grunted, then cocked his head. *Hay.* He spotted the stable and stuck his nose through an open window, a horse snuffling his head. A man stood watch over the main doors, but he was a long walk down the stone aisle.

He eyeballed the horse. "Hush now."

And he climbed, pushing sideways through gap, before slinking to the straw covered floor. He crept to an interior corner of the stall and sat with his back to the stable's aisle.

He'd traded a comfy bed for the smell of piss, shit, and hay; the sun couldn't rise soon enough.

{❊❊❊}

Maybe he dozed, but he never felt as if he slept; either way morning came with a gray light and the patter of rain. He stood in the stall, the burn in his side enough to make him forget the cramps in his legs from squatting in the corner for candles.

He glanced through the bars of the stall, and seeing no one, reached his arm through to unlatch and open the door, then slipped into the aisle. On closing, the door squealed, and his gaze turned to the end of the hall where a guard had stood last night. No one, for a flicker, then a shadow drawn by the noise appeared.

"You there. What's your business?"

Solineus straightened, hilts at his waist and hidden by the folds of his cloak. "I rode in yester-eve, just checking on the beast to make sure he's still sound."

The guard's hand was on his sword, a small-sword suitable to fighting in tight spaces, but his stride and grip didn't betray a man looking for a fight.

"We've a horse-doctor at the stables for a price, if he needs tending."

Solineus nodded and smiled as the man drew close. "I thank you… We went through some nasty terrain, got a cut on his hock. You don't have something handy, a salve for the wound? Save me a few dâguts to pay you instead of them?"

The guard's hand lifted from his sword with a chuckle. "It would at that. Come with me, I think we got some mêeru paste down here."

The man asked four dâguts for the yellow goop, and Solineus paid him five, before going back to pretend to treat the animal. Instead, he removed his makeshift bandages and applied the vile-smelling paste to himself.

He locked the stall, thanked the man for his help, and wandered into the street wondering how many guardsmen hunted a murderous foreigner this morning. Maybe none, if they recognized it as an attempt to kill him. Maybe a thousand, if they had things all wrong. Maybe it would only be Dark Waters giving him chase. Maybe he just needed to get the hells out of this city before the only thing that mattered was his being dead.

He wandered for a candle, as the only thing he knew was that the gates they'd entered were to the east; he figured walking any direction would get him to the outer walls, and from there a gate. However, straight lines in this city were harder to plot than he figured.

He found the southern gate first, but there was no one there but guards, and it remained closed. He meandered for a few wicks to see if it'd open for other folks but decided to head west rather than ask the gates open.

He pulled the hood of his cloak and kept the Twins hidden as he walked westerly, doing his best to keep an eye on the wall to keep his bearings. To his joy the gate stood open, and though guarded, the armed men glanced at passing folks but didn't ask questions nor demand hoods drawn from faces in the rain.

He spotted wagons and horsemen heading for the gate, put on a smile, and strolled west along the broad road. Horsemen clattered past him first, then he passed through the gate about the same time the wagon caught him.

Within flickers he was alone on the road, and when he passed over the crown of the first hill, he pulled a map from his haver. He traveled the Ilipsôu Road from Klondihîk, and it continued west, this was the good news. The bad news was that the road's winding trail faded and disappeared within a hundred horizons, leading into blank vellum on the map. Tanzarêu had traveled the Foundations all her life, but she'd never gone where Solineus' road took him.

FIFTEEN

Fire Dancers

Who are you to whisper words to the Uncaring Wind,
purveyor of the age-old sin,
partake and take and slake the kin.
The Slaker the Baker,
progenitors of the age-old sin,
wings of the Forlorn Wren, the hole in the den,
the awkward silent amid the deafening din.
Who is the Uncaring Wind to whisper of your end?

—*Tomes of the Touched*

Solineus stood alone atop the edge of a world changing color. Behind him rose mountains turning whiter with the coming of fall and winter, before him stood a plain still filled with greens, browns, and reds. Eighteen months in the Foundations living amongst a people who were a variety of peoples, months in hiding at the Sun Forge, and the final months to reach a new world where no one would speak a language he understood. Just how the Twelve Hells did the Lady expect him to succeed without a common tongue?

He wandered three more days, eating what he could find, whether snake, hare, or flower, and drinking water washing cold from the mountains. The land was wide-open, but its flat was a deception with ravines and ruts cutting across the landscape in a pattern born of nature's chaos. They slowed his travel, and could hide people or animals, allowing them pass day or night a hundred paces away, without his ever realizing they'd been there.

He stared at the stars while wrapped in his bedroll, a cool breeze rustling his hair, until his lids drooped and slipped toward slumber. Easy breaths and calm, until the tingle came. A zing at the base of his neck that brought his eyes open to scattered clouds. He dreamed, or someone watched him. He sat straight, one hand on the grip of the singing shield, the other finding the Sister's hilt by his side.

The remnants of his fire were an ember's glow, and the moon hid under a heavy cloud to leave him lost in a dark night. He looked around, squinting, but if anything was out there, he sure the hells couldn't see it. Sister clicked as he tugged the hilt, and her whispers rushed into his mind, but it was the creak of a bow's string which drew his attention. A fight with an invisible enemy wasn't going to end well. He shoved the sword back into its sheath and raised his hand.

The Dark Waters believed him dead, and they'd carry crossbows. He spoke in Kingdomer, hoping for a common tongue. "Peace."

A glint in the dark caught his eye as the cloud covering the moon passed; an arrowhead. And the man behind it was big, too big to be human. The voice was a deep rumble: "Îyombarê Purêlô."

"I don't understand."

He drew closer, until Solineus' eyes made out a furry beast with a mane, big eyes that reminded him of the mountain lions of the Foundations. An Ilu-Silvstro.

"Têumharâ?

"Shits." And the bowstring creaked again, the arrow at rest long enough to put through two men. *What the hells was that word Ivin said?* "*Gostelium finshol?*"

"*Gostelium finshol? Humotru?*" A voice came from behind, and Solineus jerked in start. These folks were quiet as the godsdamned Edan.

"Just… *Gostelium finshol.*" He raised both hands in what he hoped they'd recognize as a gesture of frustrated peace and spoke in every language he knew. "Kingdomer, Silone, Edan."

"You speak Ilu-Shiludân?"

He turned to the woman's voice. He'd never heard the words before… yet he understood them. *How the hells?* Understand them or not, the words were difficult for his tongue to form. "I do. It seems."

The tension of the bowstrings eased, and he breathed easier. The woman sat beside his fire pit, and it flared to life; green eyes glowed in the light, observing him with a cat's dispassionate gaze. "Who are you to be on the Plains of the Ilu?"

"I am Solineus Mikjehemlut, of the Clan Emudar, of the Silone people."

"We know nothing of these names. Why are you here?"

"I've crossed the Foundations all the way from Helmveline to the east, seeking friends and now the city of Mulshuhar."

"Clanemudar—"she ran the words together"—Hundred Nations?"

His eyes flew open. "No! No. An island further north."

"If you hale from a land so far away, how is it you know Ilu-Shiludân?"

Oh hells. He exhaled, scratched his forehead. "I picked it up in the Kingdom of Barkûsh, from traders there."

"No."

Bows creaked, at least four of them. "You're right. But you won't believe me." She stared, and he knew then he wouldn't want to play cards with this woman. "I don't have the slightest idea. I can speak Edan. How? I don't know." He shrugged.

"Yes." A toothy smile and the strings eased again. "This is peculiar, but you do not lie. Clanemudar? Who are your allies and enemies?"

"Enemies… the Hundred nations, every damned one far as I know. Allies, the Trelelunin, Helmveline, the Silone clans, all allies: The Ravinrin, Choerkin—"

"Choerkin?" Her furry head cocked, her glowing eyes blinking as they looked to her friends around camp. "Choerkin? Ivin Choerkin?"

Son of a bitch. He threw his hands in the air with a big smile. "Ivin Choerkin! One of my best allies. He's marrying my daughter."

The woman grabbed him so quick he'd have been gutted before he could flinch if she wanted; instead, she hugged him, butted her forehead to his, then licked his cheek with a tongue so rough it damned near hurt. She didn't let go, and the others took turns walking by to lay their hands on his shoulders.

"Ivin Choerkin, a good man."

"Yes, he saved… The Ilu-Silvstro he befriended made it home?" Stupid question once spoken aloud, but he was too happy to care.

"Yes. His name has spread through all the families. I am called Yumûlu, you may name me friend. Come!" She jumped to her feet, dragging him with her with such strength his toes left the ground several fingers. "The Pride of Mêolu welcomes you to our hunting grounds and our war! Run with us and feast."

"War? What do you mean war?" He picked up the Twins and his shield, slinging them over his shoulders.

Her fanged smile unnerved him with its joy. "You said the Hundred Nations are your enemy?"

Me and my mouth. "I did…"

"Then you're at war! Run with us."

He knelt and rolled his bed, stood with it and his pack. He scoffed and muttered in Silone. "War. Forges take me."

When he stood, she arched her shoulders and screamed, a sound blending cougar's call with a Kingdomer song. Haunting. And at least a dozen more voices screamed from the dark, a sound which put a shiver through his core.

A godsdamned war party. Guess I should be grateful they're not at war with the Choerkin. "We run."

He didn't expect she meant literally, but by the Twelve Hells was he wrong. He sprinted to catch up with their loping, springy gait. "Woah, woah, woah! You want me to go to war you best slow down." Still he needed to trot to keep pace, and he prayed their camp wasn't more than a couple horizons distant, or his heart might burst before finding a battle.

❋❋❋

Blazing fires licking poles high burned on a midnight horizon with flailing shadows milling around. Solineus' first thought went straight to battle, but it didn't feel right… then that the bodies of the fallen were burning. Wrong on both accounts.

The fires burned on a red-rock hill swept bare by winds and rain, and Ilu-Silvstro paraded around the fires dancing and singing. Some thrust bows or arrows into the air, other swords with blades long as spears. More disturbing were those who whirled ropes strung with what he guessed were human skulls.

His grasp of the language was tenuous, and he hadn't a clue what these people sang.

Yulûmu and her people jumped straight into the mix of dancers, but Solineus stood with shifting feet before backing away. The puncture in his side throbbed after the run to get here, and on top of that, the notion of getting knocked around in a dance where everyone had claws and outweighed him by twenty bricks didn't appeal to his preservation instinct.

Yulûmu peeled from the mix of dancers and leaped to stand in front of him with a fanged smile. "You do not dance?"

He coughed. "No. I don't. And I have a wound."

"A wound? You should've told me. Where?" He pointed to his side and she lifted his arm and armor with a yank, spun him to look at his back. "The cut healing, but we should clean this other and treat it."

Her grip kept his arm and he didn't have a choice but to follow where she led. They passed five bonfires before arriving at a yurt fashioned from wooden poles and some thick hide. Six cots sat out front, four of them with Ilu stretched across them.

She pointed to an empty cot. "Remove your cloak and armor. Lay on your stomach, I'll be back in a flicker."

He wandered to the fur-covered cot, high enough it came close to his waist, and crawled atop after stripping his armor. The other Ilu sprawled on these things were huge men, he guessed seven feet tall and were double his weight if not more; he felt a bit like a child atop the fur-covered contraption, but it wasn't uncomfortable after a couple hours of running.

He closed his eyes and relaxed into the heavy fur blanket. Until something wet struck his back.

He jumped and rolled; Yumûlu sat beside him, her tongue out and a peevish cast to her eyes. "You licked me."

"Lay still." He didn't have much choice as her fingered paw shoved him back down. Her tongue stretched his wound several times, its texture rough and painful. "You fear you taste so good I'll eat you?"

He laughed as her tongue hit his back again. "I hope the hells not."

"I wouldn't eat you alive anyhow, nor raw, unless in a pinch."

These people had a sense of humor. He hoped. Then the cold hit the wound like a block of ice, and he yelped. "Holy hells." The cold turned warm, then hot enough he wondered if the ice hadn't turned into an ember. "What the hells are you doing to me?"

"Healing you. What are these hells? We Ilu know only one hell."

"Lucky you, I think I just experienced two with that concoction you slapped on me."

She laughed and slapped him in the back of his head with a paw the size of his face; soft but forceful at the same time. "You are a funny man."

Her eyes darted into the night, and Solineus followed the gaze, fearing the war had arrived, but with the fires blazing all around he saw nothing but darkness. "What is it?"

"Rêmwûer and his pride, I believe. You can't see them?"

Solineus squinted. "With the fires here, no."

"You are weak and blind. Good to know."

He snorted. "I'm not blind… it's the fires and the night."

It wasn't long before he spotted figures running toward them, and Yumûlu waved and shouted: "Rêmwûer!"

A gigantic Ilu, with a mane so full it was twice Solineus' chest, trotted to them and hugged her. His fur was a golden tan like a mountain lion, and human skulls dangled from a gold chain around his neck, the backs of the skull cut off, so they lay flat against his chest.

He glanced at Solineus along with the hollow eyes of dead men dangling from his neck. "You caught a Tek and heal him?"

She swatted his shoulder, hard enough Solineus figured he might've stumbled if hit so hard. "He is Solineus of the Clanemudar, friend of Ivin Choerkin."

"Clan Emudar."

Rêmwûer raised his head and roared, much like a great cat. "Friend of Ivin! You will war with us tomorrow! You will lose, but still have fun."

"Lose! I'd much rather win." But he was already beginning to think his grip on their language was softer than he thought.

The man-lion leaned to pinch his arm, claws retracted. "These are not the muscles of a victor, Little-Furless. But war is fun."

Solineus sat up on his cot. "Just what is this war you're talking about?"

"We run, jump, demonstrate are expertise with bows and spears and javelins, many wars of strength and agility! We practice to kill the Hundred Nations!"

Solineus breathed easier and laughed. "Games! I will game with you as much as you like, even if I should lose. Fun!"

Both Ilus roared.

"But if I'm going to be worth a damn, I need some food."

Yumûlu nodded. "My apologies, Little-Furless. Antelope, you prefer raw or cooked?"

"Cooked. Really cooked, no red." It pleased him to know food was on the way, but his new nickname would take some getting used to.

Sixteen

Red Dirt to Red Domes

Hearts of children beat with whispers of promise,
the hollowed drum eager for living yet seen.
Hearts of elders beat with whispers of wisdom,
the ruptured drum spilling a past soon forgotten.
Hearts of between mistake morsels for meals,
too satiated to be hungry,
too empty to be full.
Too ignorant to grasp wisdom,
too wise to realize ignorance.
Certainty is the Fool's conundrum.

—*Tomes of the Touched*

The dawn arrived in silence. Everyone in Yumûlu's yurt still slept, and when he slipped out to find a bush to step behind, he found the entire camp sleeping in. His wound was cooled to the touch, any infection gone, so he sat and waited for the Ilu to rise.

A half candle later a roar came from the east, a mighty sound that no doubt carried for a horizon. Within a wick the entire camp bustled with lions laughing and enjoying breakfast. It was a good thing he enjoyed meat, because they didn't offer him so much as a sprig of vegetable.

A turkey leg. Or rather, the leg of the biggest damned bird he ever imagined, dripped grease on his boots as he ate; delicious, and with so much meat on the bone he couldn't eat it all.

The Ilu didn't eat, they devoured, putting down pounds of flesh by the time he could spot the bone beneath his leg of bird, and soon as they were finished, they left him, trotting down into the valley.

All except Yumûlu, who stared at him, that emotionless stare so common of cats, but in this case, he could actually ask and expect an answer. "What?"

"Are you going to eat that or play with it?"

He stammered. "Fine, I'll save this for lunch."

She jumped to her feet and strode after the others, leaving him to trot to catch her. She led him to an open field where thirty or more Ilu stood around with longbows in hand. Every one of them wore a necklace of human skulls, some painted in garish reds and blues, while others remained bleached white; he had to remind himself they belonged to Teks, not his own kin.

Yumûlu said, "These are the warriors who qualified in our archery contest. There are three ranges."

Solineus gazed in the direction she pointed. The first target was about a hundred strides away, the second twice that, and the third… "Are you shittin' me?" She stared, with no idea what he'd said. He coughed. "That's a long way. No comments about my muscles."

A purring chuckle rumbled in her throat, and within a wick the games began. Arrows flew, Ilu tallied scores with scratches on a board, and they moved through the first two rounds with great speed.

Rêmwûer held a score of seventy-two, putting him in third place from what he gathered. The massive lion strode their way and handed Solineus his bow and an arrow.

Solineus grinned, raised the bow, and tested the string, drawing it as far as his lip before surrendering. "I lose."

Roars of laughter. "This is a gift for you, Little-Furless! It will train your muscles."

"I'll need shorter arrows." No way he'd draw long as Rêmwûer did even if he had the strength, his arms were too short.

The Ilu nodded and walked away.

"I thought there were three rounds?"

"Different bows."

Solineus turned back and Rêmwûer snatched another bow from a rack, this one heavier still, and long as a spear. He dropped to his back and put the bow to his feet before nocking an arrow, drew back with a roar. Waited. Then let fly. The arrow burst from the string with a rush. Hard as the hells to see it in the sky despite its size.

"Son of a bitch." A quarter of a horizon at least, but he couldn't tell if Rêmwûer had hit the target.

The man jumped to his feet and stared into the distance. Flickers later a roar from the target area, and he raised his hands to cheers.

Solineus found it difficult to believe an arrow so big could fly so far, and with precision (although Yumûlu told him the targets were twenty hands around). Near half the archers hit the target, and in the end Rêmwûer took second place.

For his part, Solineus was happy as the hells Rêmwûer had been joking about his playing in the games, there was no way to compete. They ran sprints, jumped posts, leaped over each other standing in rows, threw javelins and spears, lifted boulders, tossed boulders, climbed poles, leaped to scratch high on poles, leaped from pole to pole like they were squirrels in trees, and after dark they topped it with a beer drinking contest, in which everyone was allowed to compete. No shock that he lost the one event he was allowed to play in.

He sat splay-legged in front of a bonfire, leaning against a log with a horn of beer jammed into the ground in front of him, wondering if he would belch or throw-up next. He closed his eyes, accepting his fate in whichever direction.

Neither. He just *suffered.*

Yumûlu found him as he sat staring at the horn, eased next to him, and offered him a greasy bite of bird. "Oh gods, no thank you." Her purr-chuckle rumbled beside him, shaking his skull until he grimaced. "That's strong beer."

"It is. There is a spirit-smoke tomorrow. Rêmwûer wonders if you would like to join us."

"Is that before or after I die tonight?"

A fanged smile. "High sun tomorrow."

He blinked, his lids slow and doing little to sooth his burning and blurred eyes. "I might recover by then. What is it?"

"Victors of each competition gather with kin and friends in a yurt. We burn the holy fire and slip into spirit dreams to seek guidance. To honor you and Ivin Choerkin. Do your people believe in such things?"

His head wobbled as he turned to look at her. "My people don't, but I sure the hells do. I would be honored to join your spirit-smoke tomorrow."

"This is good, I feared you might say no."

He laughed. "If I did, would my head become jewelry?"

"No, heads are in earned in war. Yours would be kicked around in children's games before thrown away." Her fanged smile was impossible to interpret.

"Good to know." He grinned, choosing to believe her words another joke. "I hope it's good that I sleep right here tonight." He patted the ground.

She leaped to her feet. "We call these celebrations *shezmûtû-doyo,* 'sleep where you fall' nights. I will bring you a fur in case the night grows chill."

By the time he woke he wasn't sure if he'd muttered his thank you, but he knew he'd meant to. The fur was warm, the ground was hard, and his head banged with the ferocity of a war drum. He pulled the cover over his head, grateful the skin was thick enough to black-out the morning sun. Yumûlu was more difficult to hide from.

She pulled the fur from his face and shoved a horn to his lips. "Drink."

His stomach gurgled and he tried to pull his blessed shadow back over his eyes, but her grip was strong. "Drink, then you can have your fur back."

He snorted and drank; it tasted like a honey-water and went down easy enough. He covered his eyes and within flickers the growl in his gut eased. He languished in his agony, and he must've dozed, for when he opened his eyes again, he felt human. A throb rested behind his eyes, but he grew courageous enough to throw off the blanket.

He looked around, noting quite a few Ilu still stretched across the ground. At least he wasn't the last one to rise. "You live." Yumûlu's voice came from behind, the start she gave his heart making his head pound again.

He crawled to his feet. "Rumor speaks it so, but I'm not certain."

"The spirit-smoke will let you know whether you are alive or dead. Come."

He looked to the sky, and damned if the sun was approaching its zenith. "I need food."

"There is no food before the spirit-smoke."

"Hells, just kill me now."

She laughed, but neither fed nor killed him. Instead she led him to a large yurt, its roof already spewing smoke, where Rêmwûer and fifteen other Ilu awaited him.

"Little-Furless! I heard you might miss the spirit-smoke while praying your guts into the dirt."

Solineus assumed the man meant vomiting. "I am nothing if not resilient."

Lion laughter roared, and Rêmwûer led them through the tent's flap. Inside was dark but for a fire burning in a brass brazier shaped as a lion's head, only it sported four faces. He stuck close to Yumûlu through the haze of smoke and took a seat beside her.

She leaned into his ear. "Just relax and follow along."

A woman stepped to stand behind Rêmwûer, her golden fur painted in streaks of blues and reds, and she wore a crown of wildflowers over an intense stare. She hissed with fangs bared, then raised her arms, her voice rising in a chant, then sinking low. She dipped her fingers into pouches at her waist and streaked Rêmwûer's forehead and cheeks in red and blue that matched her own markings. She danced around the fire, fingers touching everyone's faces to leave their marks, and after each, she sprinkled dust into the fire. Her fingers rubbed Solineus' face and he could feel the claws even if they didn't hook or slice him. And when she turned, sprinkling dust in the fire, for the first time he saw smoke rise in hues of blue and red, mingling into purples.

The roof's chimney closed, and the smoke grew thick, and he closed his eyes against the burn. But his lungs breathed easy. The throb in his head from the night's drinking disappeared. He relaxed and sat straight, and his eyes opened without a burn.

Everyone but the priestess sat stone-still, and she danced and chanted, her motions floating and slow, her words stretched. He understood phrases now, or rather grasped a hint of their meaning: She prayed to Ferinmufûer, the Great Pride Father, and beseeched the Wisdom of the Ancestors for his children gathered here. She laid a hand to Rêmwûer's forehead and pushed, and the powerful man fell backward as a feather floating to the ground. One after the other the Ilu toppled at her touch, until her blue-powdered paw pressed the bridge of his nose and covered his eyes.

He heard her blessing and felt himself fall, but never felt a landing. He plummeted into a smiling eternity where there was no bodily pain nor grieving. Paradise. Until he opened his eyes to a world of blue.

The place was familiar, the same, but different. The swirling blues were darker, and the grays carried tints of smoky-red.

"Hello, my love."

He opened his mouth to speak, but all he managed was a laugh. The Lady appeared before him, hovering and beautiful, but he swore her face was furry and whiskered. He laughed more. "What lion heaven am I in?"

She frowned, or smirked, it didn't matter, he continued to laugh either way. "The Ilu have only one heaven and one hell. The spirit-smoke has taken your wits, my love."

He snorted a breath and regained a modicum of composure. "Aye, aye, I… Damn."

She sighed, faded, and reappeared by his side. A warm hand rose, rubbing his cheeks and forehead. "You've traveled slower than I expected. You need to head west."

A sense of normality seeped into his being with her by his hide, and the real world returned to his thoughts. "The city of red domes. Mulshuhar."

"This is what people call it now? You have time, but the sooner you travel the better." She hovered above him, her face now the same as it had ever been. Perfect.

"How can my past await me in Mulshuhar?" Something scratched his back, at the same time as his collar choked stretched his neck.

The Lady smiled. "Travel and find out."

He awoke with a rushing breath of fresh air, his chest being crushed, and with a view of Yumûlu leaning over him. She stopped pushing his chest. "You live!"

"Think you broke a rib or two, but yes." He rolled to his side and coughed, but she grabbed his head and turned it back to her.

"Your markings are gone."

Solineus recalled the Lady rubbing his face and forehead. Did she have the power to affect his body from the blue universe? He gazed up at her huge leonine eyes, so similar and different than the Lady in his dreams. "My spirit guide took them." His head spun when he coughed.

She gasped. "You traveled to the spirit realm as I did?"

"I did. What did you see?"

"The Hunting Fields and the Great eagle Filûrêu, the Huntress of Sky and Plains."

He smiled, having expected her spirit guide to be a feline. "What did this eagle say?"

"She told me to awake, to drag you from the tent and save your life. Who was your guide? What did they say?"

His heart beat slow. "I don't know her name. She told me to travel to Mulshuhar to find… myself."

She tilted her head to the sky, arms raised, and claws flicking from her fingers. "Praise the Pride Father for giving you the destination of all dreamers."

Solineus sat up, unnerved by her claws despite himself. "That's all well and good, but it'd be handy if she told me where the hells the city is at."

Yumûlu's claws retracted and she glanced at him as if he was a fool. "Everybody knows where Mulshuhar is."

He rolled onto his back and chuckled. "Throw me onto a cart and drag me there. Not sure I can walk anymore."

❊❊❊

Yumûlu and Rêmwûer announced their engagement later in the day, and much drinking followed again that night, but Solineus practiced the wisdom he'd learned with the Kingdomers and claimed a bellyache to get himself as far from the kegs as he could get.

The next morning Solineus walked surrounded by a handful of Ilu, including the engaged couple. The Ilu took his spirit guide's words to heart when he spoke of hurrying, and they only stopped to sleep. For twenty-six days they strode the red rock lands at a pace that taxed his body and spirit, but as the land shifted from reds to browns and grays they came upon what Yumûlu called the Mulshuhar road. Here they stopped and waited, sitting on a hill overlooking the road.

Horses and carts traveled from the south in regular intervals, but it took a candle for a wagon to come rolling in from the north. Two mules pulled a family, but the man was nowhere near the size of Ilpen.

Rêmwûer trotted to the road and raised his paw, and Solineus didn't know whether the wagon would stop, or turn and run. Within a wick, they were waved to to the road.

Yumûlu said, "Come. He has a ride for you."

They strolled down the hill and she spoke to the man in a language Solineus couldn't understand.

He looked to Rêmwûer. "It has been an honor to walk with you."

"And you! Little-Furless."

"If ever you meet more of my people, show them the kindness you've shown me. Don't wear any of their skulls?"

He nodded with a grin. "I will or won't." And he laughed with a roar. "Maybe someday I will share a spirit-smoke with your Ivin Choerkin."

Solineus clasped forearms with the man, and Rêmwûer leaned in to butt his forehead; a ring between his ears ensued, but the big cat meant well.

Next, he turned to Yumûlu, and she spoke. "This is Kîger and his bride Mêlsok, their children Kêtû and Bolris. They are Ergôtrîts and know only a few Kingdomer words, but they will carry you to Mulshuhar." She grabbed both his arms and butted his head; he should've worn his helmet.

He blinked the concussion away. "Thank you. May you two live long together and build a pride worthy of your names."

She cocked her head with a toothy smile, her giant tongue lolling over one fang. "That was a very good blessing, Little-Furless, I think the spirit-smoke raised your Ilu soul. You return to us one day, Solineus of the Clanemudar."

"I will. I've a lot of returning to do, may as well make this another stop." He climbed onto the back of the wagon, and with a snap of the reins the mules pulled him away from yet another set of new friends.

He smiled.

The first new friends where no one was left behind dead.

Seventeen

Future's Witness Past

Tantrums thrown and tantrums crashed,
the willing waiting did treasure amass.
Wondering wandering wonders,
the bloated dead man's blunders.
A stab, a stoke, a murderous pig in a poke,
the deception in sight,
to build the weakness in your own might.
Might, maybe, seeing sight the might,
the fight outside of fright.

— *Tome of the Touched*

The family he traveled with shared about fifty words in the Kingdomer tongue with him, simple things like eat and sleep, but after a week of bouncing in the back of their wagon, he heard words he'd been waiting for: "Mulshuhar close, now."

He perked up, excited for the next candle or two. They rolled along a stretch of road a hundred strides from massive cliffs that fell into the sea, or Kônu Bay, as they named it. To the south its bright blue waters stretched to the horizon, and to the north a land of oranges, browns, and greens. The air was warm and dry, and if not for swarms of bugs wanting to suck his blood, he figured he might've found a version of paradise. But, the red domes of the city were nowhere in sight by the time they bedded down for the night.

The next morning Kîger said it again: "Mulshuhar close, now."

This time he yawned and nodded, but by midmorning their wagon nosed into a slope headed for the sea, and on the horizon red-gold domes shown in the sun with an astounding glow. He'd never seen a city so beautiful, so huge, so pristine. "Son of a bitch… I made it." He checked his tongue; he wasn't there yet. But after damned near two years since blowing the bridge… had it been so long? Not yet, but close enough for him to accept the rounding error. Two years to reach this city in the hopes the Lady in his dreams wasn't full of shit.

He chuckled to himself and the family turned to stare, yapping between themselves about something.

He stood and balanced with legs spread, the extra height enough to see a hundred ships harbored. The wagon bounced and he took a seat, sharing a laugh with the family.

Mulshuhar was beyond beautiful, it was stunning, a city fashioned from stone a hundred shades of umber, ranging from light-golden to roasted chestnut, and either polished to a shine or rough cut. Houses and buildings sat capped by roofs of green or red tiles, but rising from its center was the *Mehul-Shundelâ*, the Palace of Red Domes, where every stone was a polished golden-umber and its three dozen towers sported glowing crowns of a deep, rose-gold.

Winds rolled in brisk and warm from Kônu Bay, and as they wheeled down the sloping city toward the harbor, he found himself floundering to imagine how many people lived her. A wild array of people lined the streets in more fashions than he'd imagined, and the peoples ranged from loud and boisterous to wrapping their heads to hide their faces. But no matter what they looked like or how they dressed, the thing which boggled his mind was how many of them there were.

The wagon stopped outside a long warehouse with a lurch, and Kîger and his family climbed from their seats, waving for him to climb down. "Here. Here. Done."

Solineus stepped to the man and smiled, slipped a silver dâgut into his hand. "Thank you." And he bowed.

Kîger held the coin up. "No, no."

"No?" Was the man unhappy with the gift? He offered another coin but Kîger smiled and waved it away.

"No dâgut. Smedên." He reached into a pocket and pulled out a tiny coin, but its color spoke all Solineus needed to know: Red gold. Local coinage.

Solineus laughed and smiled with a nod. "Smedên, where can I exchange coins?"

"*Te te te…*" The man pointed, then huffed before turning to his son. "Zêgu! *Tompolê eñeû far rôchu.*"

The boy rolled his eyes but that was as close as he came to defying his father. He stomped down the street and Solineus followed after bowing again to Kîger and his wife.

They crossed three broad streets and descended four steep stairs, then strode a half horizon down a street that never ceased being crowded. Again he wondered how damned many people were in this place. Tens of thousands was about the extent of his imagination.

Zêgu stopped and pointed to a building marked by a wooden sign painted with four coins. Solineus slipped the boy a few dâguts, and he smiled, no longer irritated his father had sent him with the foreigner. "Thank you."

The boy bowed and bounded east, and Solineus strode into the coin exchange. The streets were crowded, but fewer than a dozen souls stood visible in this posh room. Rugs of matching and intricate geometric weaves covered much of the floor, but where the stone showed, it was polished orange marble, and the desks were carved from rosewood if he guessed right. He felt out of place in his armor and the Twins riding his back, and the workers here agreed, caring not a wit for his presence so far as he could tell, and he wondered if unwrapping the Ikoruv hilts of the Twins might change their minds. But he chose patience, standing in the soft breeze of a giant fan spinning above.

Several wicks later a tap landed on his shoulder, and he turned to face a woman short enough and squat enough to be a Kingdomer, but she was pudgy rather than powerful. She did her best to smile. "Hedû?"

"You speak Kingdomer?"

"Yes, I do."

Her accent was funny, but it was damned nice to understand someone again. "I need to exchange some dâguts for smedên."

"Yes. Of course. This way. There will be a three percent fee for any exchange."

She led him to a table and sat, but she didn't offer him a seat. He reached into his pack and pulled out his pouch with Morik's gift in it, untied it, and placed it in front of her. She sighed and pulled it to her with a disinterested grin, glanced inside, and her eyes didn't leave for what felt a wick. When she looked up it wasn't to him. "Ket! Ket!"

A man standing nearby hustled away, and Solineus' heart beat fast. *What the hells?* Then he felt a chair pushed against the back of his legs.

"Please, sit." She reached into the pouch and pulled out coins, thick and silver, some thin and gold, and she built stacks from them. "Did you come to Mulshuhar to buy a ship?"

His head jerked as if from a spasm. *Buy a ship?* He swallowed, not certain what the hells to say. How much had the Kingdomer given him? Then he looked closer: the edges of one golden stack held a violet tint. Timôu, infused gold. He coughed. "I was considering it."

"Good!" She laughed. "We can't exchange such an amount… not until tomorrow. You will need to sign some papers, a statement of value… and how you came by this wealth?"

He nodded, keeping calm, no reason to raise undeserved suspicion. "That is well enough. King Sînhôlar the Ironwing, of the Kingdom of Helmveline, gifted me this sum for performing a task."

She slouched in her seat and eyeballed him. "You've some proof? A writ or statement?"

He removed his pack and burrowed his hand to the bottom, pulling out the griffon cloak. "I have this." He shook it out and draped it over a shoulder.

She rose in her seat with a smile and a cough. "The king of… Well! This will take some time to document. We will make it clear you are an agent of Helmveline, this will speed things. We can exchange the silver and gold now if you'd like?"

"That is well."

She snapped her fingers and a man placed a tray covered with stacks of smedên on the table. She started counting. "You aren't of Helmveline, how did you come to serve the Ironwing?"

"That is a story too long and sad to tell."

She nodded. "We'll need your name for the documents?" Her voice was so smiley and pleasant now it made him want to laugh. He figured she might collect some small part of the exchange fee.

"Solineus Mikjehemlut."

She blinked and cocked her head. "A Mikjehemlut, of the Emudar?"

His heart hit his throat, and it took a flicker before he could speak. "Yes."

"From the deep north, yes, we've had dealings with the Emudar on several occasions over the past decade."

"You have?" He rocked back in his seat, staring. "Who?"

"Oh, goodness, I don't remember every foreigner's name!" And she laughed. "Which raises the question of how in the world you came so far from the north to meet the Ironwing, and then somehow travel all the way here?"

"Dumb luck, I suspect."

She laughed again, then lay the Timôu coins in neat rows and covered them with a thin paper. She passed over them with a charcoal stick, flipped them, and did so again. "Sign here, and here." She flipped the sheet, so he signed both sides. Then the man brought a scale, and weighed the coins in order, denoting their weight on the sheet. Her brow sweated and she clucked each time she dropped a coin on the scale.

"That it? What're they worth?"

She blinked. "Hmm? Well. A quarter million smedên at the very least." Her giggle was nervous. "You are a very rich man, Lord Mikjehemlut."

"I am?" The notion felt peculiar. The five thousand four hundred and thirty-two smedên she'd given him for the regular coins had felt a fortune flickers before.

She touched his hand. "I'm single." She laughed. "Just kidding! But I could be. I'm not kidding about that." And she winked.

And the man who'd brought the tray said, "And I wouldn't even blame her for leaving me."

He glanced between the two. They laughed, and he joined in, relieving a strange pressure in his gut.

"Ho! Well, my being a wealthy man, where might I find an inn?"

They looked to one another and the man answered. "The *Golden Swordfish* is expensive but popular with the wealthiest merchants."

Solineus shook his head. "I don't need gold forks, but I don't want no rats in my bed neither."

She answered this time. "The *Timber and Nest,* two blocks straight south, on your southern-right. You won't miss it."

"Thank you." The talk of wealth faded, and his mind turned. "You mentioned Emudar… Have you seen any of my people recently?"

"No, can't say I have, but then I don't visit the docks and I've only dealt with them once personally. So many foreign ships and traders…" She shrugged.

"I thank you. Both of you." He grinned and strode from the bank exchange standing tall and a little bemused by how life turned in peculiar circles. His strides took him to and past the *Timber and Nest Inn* and all the way to the wharf's docks and its array of ships.

Not one, but four, Luxun banners snapped in the wind. Docked near each other, he couldn't resist checking to see if the *Entiyu Emoño* sat tied off. She and her captain weren't there, but what he really looked for was any sign of a Silone vessel.

The length of the wharf and docks made him swear he'd walked a horizon in one direction, but once to the end he turned and began the walk back, his nerves flaring every time her heard a voice with what he figured a Tek accent.

"Son of a bitch, Solineus Mikjehemlut. I reckon I find you in the damnedest places!"

The Silone voice with an Emudar accent lurched his heart and he spun, knowing who'd found him. "Hadin Elost…" The scrawny man was as scruffy as the last time he saw him at Choerkin Fost, and his feet still bare.

But it was the face behind him that stifled his voice and brought the Lady's words back to him: *I won't tell you who you were, but who you are and who you will be awaits you far to the west, in Kônu Bay.* It was a bit like looking in a mirror.

Lord Adinvan Mikjehemlut.

"Father?"

The Serenading Swallow you say?
Oh, you cleverest of crows,
green-eyed and black-souled,
treading the charred stone once ablaze.
No, not yet.
Walkers on Fire, Walkers on Glass,
chewers of the nail to the very last,
the past, aghast.
Waltzing the field of unbreakable broken!
Burn your feet and freeze your soul,
oh don't you know, You know, you Know,
your horrifying future can only survive
because of your missed and forgotten past.

—*Tomes of the Touched*

CITY OF WHISPERS

SUNDERING THE GODS BOOK THREE

COMING WINTER 2019/20

L. JAMES RICE

If you enjoyed this book, or hate it so much you want to read more, follow me on Facebook at

https://www.facebook.com/SunderingTheGods/:

or Join my Mailing List at:

http://sunderingthegods.com/newsletter-signup/

Fan mail, hate mail, and requests to send me millions of dollars from Nigeria, may be directed to:

LJRice@SunderingTheGods.com

Additional Maps and information on the World of the Sister Continents may be found at:

LJamesRice.Com

The Sundering the Gods Saga

Book 1: Eve of Snows

Book 1.5: Meliu (A Bridge Novella)

Book 2: Trail of Pyres

Book 2.5: Solineus

Book 3: City of Whispers
Coming Winter 2019/20

www.ingramcontent.com/pod-product-compliance
Lightning Source LLC
Chambersburg PA
CBHW030425310726
48979CB00009B/1621/J

* 9 7 8 1 9 5 1 0 6 8 0 1 1 *